By Nancy M Bell

ISBN: 978-1-77145-440-7

Books We Love, Ltd.
Calgary, Alberta
www.bookswelove.com

## Dedication

*To all the animals who need rescuing and to all those who rescue them. May they all find forever homes. Especially to Lily, Gibbie, Merrily, Miley, Alex, No Name, Hector, Spook, Big Bird, Chance, Two Socks, Rhaedar and finally, the black momma dog with no name who wasn't as lucky as Storm/*

For Hilda-Mari
( hope you enjoy
the story.
Nancy M Bell.

# Chapter One

*Silent night, Holy night.* The familiar strains issued from the barn radio and hung in the frosty air. Michelle Wilson cut the strings of the hay bale which parted with a satisfying pop. The sweet scent of summer rose from the released flakes of grass and legumes.

She spared a glance out of the barn window where the storm demons hurled fistfuls of snow out of the north. *Well, it's a holy mess out there that's for sure.* The irreverent thought brought a tiny smile to her lips as she stooped to scoop up the loose flakes.

Quickly, Michelle tossed hay into the horses' stalls and checked their water. Her two barrel racers and her brother's rope horse munched contentedly on the feed. George's mare was due to foal, but appeared comfortable at the moment. Satisfied everything was in order she flicked off the light and stepped out into the blizzard that had descended on southern Alberta. She double checked the latch on the door and then bent her head into the storm, turning toward the porch lights shining dimly through the driving snow.

Michelle stomped the snow off her boots as she crossed the wide porch at the back of the house and stepped into the warmth of the mud room. She hung her coat to dry after shaking the snow from it and placed her boots near the heat vent. There was nothing worse than ice cold boots to stick your feet into before venturing out in the bitter cold. With a sense of relief, Michelle pulled the mud room door closed behind her, filled the kettle, and set it to boil.

The warm light spilled from the kitchen window onto the drifts already accumulating on the veranda. *Now, if that mare will hold off until the storm is over, I'll be happy.* Michelle poured water into the teapot and sank down into the chair behind her. The fire crackled in the cook stove which had stood in the kitchen longer than Michelle could remember. The surface of the cast iron and enamel behemoth shone with the patina of age. The memory of her grandmother baking cookies in the cavernous oven brought a smile to her face.

She rose, poured her tea, and returned to sit at the kitchen table. Unconsciously, she smoothed the embroidered cloth covering the surface. Purple prairie crocus and the red and grey of the prairie smoke flower twined around the edges mixed with green foliage. The ranch brand adorned each corner of the cloth. Gramma made it to celebrate the day the mortgage on the ranch was paid off.

"Now they're all gone, except me and George." Michelle whispered. She missed him, even though he was a typical bossy big brother. The man always had to have things his way. Came from running a drilling crew she guessed.

She shook her head and pushed back from the table. It was no night to be wallowing in memories. The power was sure to go out with this storm, so she brought the oil lamps down from the top of the buffet in the dining room and set two on the sideboard in the kitchen. She placed another by the foot of the stair and then ventured out into the chilly wood shed attached to the front hall. No need to freeze to death fetching wood, Grandpa always said. Michelle knew he built it especially so her grandma wouldn't have to go outside in the cold to haul wood through the snow drifts when she was pregnant. Gramma always maintained ranching was man's work. The house including wood and water was her domain.

Michelle stopped for a moment and sighed. Why couldn't she find a man who would be a partner and a friend? She wanted what her grandparents had—a real team that worked together like a well-oiled machine. Grandpa always said those words with the special smile reserved for Gramma alone.

Michelle gathered the wood and paused, her foot raised to kick the door closed. She cocked her head and listened. An insistent sharp cry overrode the whine of the wind in the cracks and the hydro wires. She kicked the door shut and latched it before she entered the front hall and made her way to the living room where she dumped the armful into the wood box by the fireplace. She needed another load for the kitchen stove, but first, Michelle went to investigate the source of the cry.

Bundled against the storm once more, she waded through the drifts on the wide porch, straining to hear over the wail of the wind. Snow flung itself in her face, and Michelle blinked rapidly to clear her eyes. The snow was drifted over the edge of the porch, and she missed the top step all together, landing face first in a hard packed bank at the bottom of the stairs. Muttering words her grandma would not have been proud of, Michelle dug her way out of the hole she was mired in. She wallowed over to the edge of the porch and grabbed the bottom of the rail to pull herself onto her feet. Michelle hesitated, half in and half out of the snow bank. Yes, there it was again, the sharp insistent cry coming from under the porch. Michelle let go of the railing and dug in the snow piled up against the edge of the porch. She managed to create a tunnel large enough to wriggle through and wished she had been bright enough to bring a flashlight. It was dark as the bottom of a well under the boards of the porch floor. Michelle wriggled out again and retrieved a flashlight from inside the front door and crawled back into the hole. The beam cut a small path through the darkness and finally, at the very back, up against the side of the house, the flash of an animal's eyes reflected the light back at her.

"Hey, missy," Michelle crooned in a soft voice, the same tone she learned from her grandfather when training young horses. "What have you gone and done to yourself?"

Michelle kept up a steady conversation with the animal cowered against the side of the house. Within a few feet, Michelle could make out the shivering body of a black dog...at least she hoped it was dog and not some coyote. It was hard to be sure of the colour and shape of the thing in the faint illumination provided by the flashlight.

Cautiously, Michelle inched a bit closer. The dog lowered its head and half closed its eyes as if expecting a blow. Michelle reached out a hand. The dog curled its lips back from its teeth and a low growl rumbled in its throat.

"Now, now, missy, none of that," Michelle spoke softly and reached out confidently to touch the dog's foot nearest her.

The dog rumbled again but made no move to strike, so Michelle scrunched closer to the animal. She dug in her pocket and finally managed to extricate one of Rex's left over dog treats. She held it out to the dog. The animal hesitated, looking from the treat to Michelle and back again, clearly not trusting the offering. Michelle laid the cookie on the ground by the dog's foot and sat back. The animal snatched the biscuit without taking its eyes off Michelle.

"Are you starving then, little dog?" Michelle spoke conversationally.

As she continued to speak nonsense to the dog, she took stock of what was wrong with the creature. It was obviously pregnant. The distended belly was visible even in the dim light. A front leg was damaged  from the way the dog was holding it, and she was criminally thin. Her hipbones and the bones of her shoulders poked up sharply through the ratty, matted coat. Michelle hunched her shoulders in her jacket. It was freezing, and her knees were cold and sore from the hard ground.

*How am I supposed to get you out of here? I'm not sitting out here all night freezing my butt off, that's for sure.*

Michelle fed the dog another cookie, backed away a few feet and set another cookie on the ground. The dog eyed her suspiciously, but apparently decided hunger was greater than her fear and dragged herself across the frozen ground toward the cookie. Michelle's breath caught in her throat. The dog was covered in matted blood, and there was a huge lump on the top of her head. The front leg was either broken or dislocated. Michelle backed up another couple of feet, and the dog followed. Slowly, they made their way to the snow tunnel. Michelle crawled out butt first into the storm. The dog stopped at the entrance and refused to come any further. Michelle laid a trail of cookies across the snow and up onto the porch to the front door. Once inside, she opened a can of beef stew and dumped it into a bowl which she set just outside the opening. She hung her snowy coat on the newel post and set her boots by the door. The wind through the open door snaked across the mat and up the legs of her wet jeans. Abandoning her post for a moment, she scurried into the kitchen to retrieve a hot drink. With her hands around a cup of hot chocolate, she settled inside on the second step near the front door and waited for the dog to make up its mind.

"It's up to you now, little dog, trust me or not," Michelle whispered to the animal still cowering under the porch.

Michelle had almost given up hope after an hour passed. The house was freezing, she'd have to shut the door soon. Rising to take her cup back to the kitchen, she paused when something brushing against the door. Carefully, she padded across the floor and inched it open further. The black dog was collapsed against the frame, a trail of blood from its frost bitten paws showed where she crawled up the stairs and over the porch.

The exhausted dog didn't possess the strength to do more than growl faintly at her. Michelle eased the door open further, and the mongrel slid down the door unto the floor of the front hall.

She grasped the hall rug and slid the shivering dog into the entryway far enough to allow her to close the door on the howling wind. The dog raised her head and tried to growl fiercely, but all that came out was a guttural whimper. Michelle dropped to her knees and scooted closer. She moved her hand and cupped the dog's lower jaw in her palm. The black dog was too cold and weak to do more than narrow her eyes and curl her upper lip. Michelle sat quietly and massaged the dog's lower jaw with her fingers while she assessed what she could of the injuries with her eyes. Lulled by the warmth of the house and the gentle touch on her head, the dog let her head drop down onto the mat. Michelle grabbed an afghan hanging on the stair rail waiting to be taken upstairs, and covered the emaciated creature with it. Making as little noise as possible, she slipped down the hall into the kitchen and put the kettle back on to boil.

Deftly, Michelle began to prepare a warm gruel, canned dog food mixed with some condensed milk, a bit of kibble left over from Rex and hot water from the kettle. Michelle's eyes misted a bit as she mixed the concoction. It was four weeks today Rex left her. She missed his happy bark when he got to ride in the truck with her and his constant presence as she went about her chores. She just hadn't got around to replacing the old guy yet, the dirt over his grave was still fresh. Well, not now, she guessed, it was covered with snow.

Michelle shook her head, left the kitchen, and headed down the wide hall to the front entry way. She paused briefly as she passed the large living room. Earlier in the week, she cleared a space for the Christmas tree, but just hadn't found the time to drag the thing in from the woodshed. Christmas was only a week away. Michelle frowned. *Oh, well maybe tomorrow.* She pushed the problem of the nonexistent

Christmas tree to the back of her mind and knelt down by the shivering dog.

The black dog's nose twitched at the scent of food, and her head came up quickly when Michelle set the bowl of mush by her. With an effort, the dog buried her muzzle in the warm food. Michelle stroked her while the dog was occupied with her food and gently tested the area over the huge lump at the back of the head. Her hand came away sticky with blood and bits of matted fur. Michelle reached up and turned on the overhead light. The dog's front leg was twisted at such an unnatural angle, she was sure it was dislocated at best and probably broken. The rest of the skinny dog was a welter of cuts and missing fur. At least she didn't look like she had the mange, a fact for which Michelle was very grateful. She left the dog on the rug eating and stepped into her office to the right of the front door past the wide staircase.

Michelle picked up the receiver and was relieved to hear the dial tone. She pressed the speed dial for Doc and dropped down into her chair. Wearily, she tilted her head back and leaned it against the headrest as she listened to the phone ring. *God, I hope you're home.* Michelle just wanted to hear Doc's rusty old voice confirm what she already expected. On the tenth ring, Mary, Doc's wife, picked up the line.

"Michelle, it's so nice to hear from you. No trouble at your place I hope," Mary said brightly.

"Hey, Mary, a stray dog just wandered onto the place, looks like someone's beaten the tar out of it. I need to ask Doc for some advice. Is he around?" Michelle sat up in her chair and scrounged for some paper and a pen under the papers on her desk.

"No, dear, Doc's out at Murray's place. That fancy cutting horse of his has colic, and he's fit to be tied. Just got back from the NFR with all his winnings and now this."

"I guess it could wait 'til morning. I just wanted to know how much pain killer I should give…she's so skinny." Michelle chewed on her bottom lip.

"Well, dear, you know I could refer you to the new vet in town. Nice boy, Doc and he are talking about throwing in together anyway. Cold nights and crazy cows are getting to be too much for Luke these days," Mary offered.

Michelle smiled in spite of herself. Nobody called Doc, Luke, except his wife of forty some odd years. Just as quickly a frown clouded her features. She plain didn't like the new "boy" as Mary called him. He wasn't a rancher. He was a fancy horse guy from what she heard about him. Used to dealing with all those expensive show jumpers and people with more money that brains.

"It can wait 'til Doc gets home," she assured Mary.

"Happens that Cale is here right now and says he can stop by on his way home," Mary said in that voice of hers she used when some plan she concocted was starting to work out.

"I can't think that I'm on anybody's way home." Michelle laughed.

The ranch was ten miles out of Longview, so Michelle was confident she wasn't on the new vet's way home. Nobody other than her neighbours was likely to venture past her lane on a night like this.

Mary chuckled, and Michelle's stomach did a flip. "Silly girl, Cale bought the old Chetwynd place across the coulee from you. He's your closest neighbour now."

"Oh." Michelle's voice was small. "I haven't got around to meeting the new people yet."

"Obviously, darlin'." Mary snorted. "You can meet young Cale tonight on his way home."

"But, I…" Michelle trailed off when she realized she was talking to a dial tone. "Damn and double damn."

Michelle ran her hand over her unruly hair and sighed. Mary, bless her soul, was her mom's oldest friend. Mom was gone over five years now. With her brother, George, being away more than he was home working on the rigs, Mary had appointed herself Michelle's guardian. Michelle pushed herself out of the comfortable chair with an exasperated sigh. She knew Mary was matchmaking again. Every eligible bachelor who came into town for any length of time somehow managed to find their way to her door on some made up errand for Mary.

"Well, dog, we'll let him look you over and give us his exalted opinion, and then tomorrow I'll call Doc." Michelle spoke as she stepped out into the hall to check on the mutt.

The black dog was awake, and her mouth was open as she panted. Her body language was wary, her narrowed eyes and lowered ears indicated she didn't expect anything good to happen. At least she wasn't in any shape to charge. Michelle knelt beside the dog and offered her hand. The dog ignored the outstretched hand and continued to watch Michelle. Finally, deciding there was no threat, the dog laid its head wearily back on the rug. Michelle got to her feet and left the animal to rest. She entered the kitchen and grabbed a cloth to wipe the table with and then briskly swept the bits of hay and shavings off the floor which had fallen from her clothes. She stored the broom back its place and went to stand by the wide kitchen window, where she observed the storm was blowing as bad as ever. *If that vet doesn't have a four by, he's never getting down my lane, let alone home.* Michelle thought with some satisfaction. *Fancy city boy.*

Michelle got the bottle of aspirin out of the medicine cabinet and set it on the table. She would give the new vet until eight-thirty to put in an appearance, after that she'd give the dog one tablet. The cuts and the front leg would have to wait until she could get to Doc in the morning. She checked the clock over the sink and realized it was three hours since she checked on Liza, the buckskin mare, who was due to foal any day now. Michelle stepped quietly into the hall where the black dog was asleep with her nose resting on the lip of the bowl of food. Most of the food had vanished, and Michelle hoped it wouldn't reappear on her rug as vomit or poop. Sometimes starving animals didn't tolerate the sudden reappearance of food well.

# Chapter Two

Michelle returned to the kitchen and glanced out the window at the thick snow that was still falling. She picked up the monitor and turned the little video screen on. The mare in the barn was restless, and Michelle could see where she had kicked up straw against the walls of the stall when she laid down and got back up again. As she watched, the mare kicked at her belly and swung her head around to look at her swollen sides. The horse was young, and this was her first foal, so Michelle had no idea how she would react to another life suddenly appearing in the straw at her side.

"Great idea, George, breed the damn mare, head back to the rigs, and leave it to me to worry about foaling her out." Michelle cursed her absent brother for the millionth time.

She turned her attention back to the monitor in time to see the mare lower herself heavily to the bed of straw. Even on the grainy monitor, dark patches of sweat were apparent on the mare's neck. She set the monitor back on the table and checked on the black dog by the door one more time before she pulled on her still damp coat and crammed one of George's thick toques on her head.

The force of the wind stole her breath when she stepped out of the lee of the house. The snow was over her knees and some quickly found its way into her boots. Doggedly, Michelle plowed through the snow toward the barn. She was relieved when her hand found the rough wood of the corral fence, and she followed it to the barn. She flicked on the lights as she stepped inside. It seemed quiet after the raging wind outside, even though the old building creaked and groaned as the force of the wind hit it.

Michelle made her way quietly to where she could see into the buckskin mare's stall. The horse was down in the straw and stretched out flat on her side. Her tawny coat was dark with sweat, and her sides heaved with the strength of the contractions. Michelle stayed quiet, not wanting to disturb the mare, just be there in case she got into trouble. The woman settled herself on a bale of straw and pulled her jacket more firmly around her. Still cold, she snagged a wool cooler hanging nearby and wrapped it around herself as well.

It took the mare another thirty minutes of labour until her water broke with a gush. Michelle sat up straighter and waited. The sac and the foal should make an appearance within twenty minutes, or Michelle would have to call Mary back and see if Doc could make it out. She pushed the thought of the new vet to the back of her mind. Within ten minutes, the shiny membrane of the sac protruded from the mare, and a tiny hoof pushed against the opaque surface. The mare heaved again, and more of the foal slid into view. The tiny hoof inside the sac showed its soft rubbery bottom, complete with tiny frog as it pushed through the membrane.

"God damn it," Michelle swore as she got to her feet and unlatched the stall door. The foal was coming backward, a breech birth. "Just freaking marvellous," she muttered.

She laid her hand on the mare's haunch and moved her tail aside to check if both feet were showing. She let her breath out through her teeth at the sight of two little hind feet and two hocks laying side by side. So far so good.

"C'mon, little horse, one more push, and we should have it," Michelle encouraged the mare. "We need to get your baby out, so he can breathe."

Michelle threw her gloves into the straw and grasped the slimy hind legs of the foal and waited. When the mare convulsed with the next contraction, Michelle pulled with her, and the foal slid wetly out into the straw. Michelle tore the tough skin of the caul away from the foal's nose and face. Then she got to her feet and stepped out of the stall. The buckskin mare raised herself up off her side and peered back at the foal lying steaming on the straw behind her. Michelle held her breath, waiting for the mare to realize the foal belonged to her. A throaty nicker came from the mare's throat, and the foal struggled and kicked his way free of the caul. The buckskin heaved herself to her feet and moved to nose the small body in the bedding, soon her tongue was licking him clean and dry.

Michelle allowed herself a small sigh of relief. She slid back into the stall with a length of binder twine in her hands and spoke softly to the mare. The horse paid her no mind, and Michelle trailed her hand from the mare's shoulder to her hindquarters and lifted the heavy afterbirth which was still attached and hanging out onto the floor. She caught the heavy caul and tied it up to the mare's tail, so it wouldn't get stepped on and pull away from the mare, leaving a piece of it still attached inside. Once the afterbirth was up out of the way, Michelle left the stall again and leaned on the door to watch the momma and baby get to know each other. The buckskin pushed the foal with her nose, and the foal attempted to get his legs underneath him and stand. On his third try, he managed to scramble up on his stilt-like legs, only to fall in a heap. The next time, he had better luck, and the mare pushed him with her nose toward her flanks. The baby stuck his nose under her flank and found the udder. Michelle held her breath. This was the moment when some first time mothers objected strongly to the foal groping around her swollen and tender udder. The sound of slurping and the mare's tongue licking the foal's butt was music to her ears. His little tail twitched as he ate his first meal. Right now, she needed a hot drink, even though she'd have to come out later and make sure the baby had his first poop and passed the meconium out of his system. The first bowel movement was sticky, thick and dark. If he didn't pass it, the colt would need an enema.

Michelle left the pair to settle and flicked the lights off as she left. She pulled her toque down further over her ears and squinted through the heavy curtain of snow, trying to see the glow of the porch light. The veils of wind-whipped snow obscured any chance of her actually seeing the light, so Michelle put her hand on the corral fence, and using it as a guide, headed in the direction she knew the house was. She came to the end of the corral and could make out the bulk of the garage just ahead of her. Stepping into the lee of the building she paused to catch her breath and wipe the snow from her face.

"Almost there," she muttered through cold lips. "Stupid snow storms," she added as an afterthought.

Michelle struck out from the shelter of the garage with her chin tucked down on her chest. The corner of the house should be right in front of her. The wind howled fiercely, and snow devils whirled everywhere, throwing biting bits of ice into her face. Her feet found the steps of the back porch first, and Michelle thankfully grabbed the snowy railing with her right hand. The drifts were thick on the broad steps and made it hard to get footing. Michelle fought her way up the stairs and missed the top step. She pitched head first into the big drift on the porch between the steps and the door. Michelle floundered in the snow as she tried to find some purchase for her feet in the sifted snow. Her breath stuck in her throat as her flailing hand was caught in the grasp of a strong gloved hand.

"George, is that you? What are you doing home? Is the rig shut down?" Michelle gasped as she used the extended hand as an anchor and emerged from the snow.

She got to her feet and pushed the snow laden toque back from her eyes and swiped her wet hair out of her face. Her eyes widened in surprise as she looked up at the tall figure of a man who was definitely not George. The porch light behind the stranger made it hard to see his features, that and the fact he had a hat pulled low over his face and a scarf wound around his neck and lower face. *Who the hell is he?* A small jolt of fear seared through her. This was definitely not someone she knew. *Maybe somebody stranded by the blizzard?*

"Michelle?" The man's voice was barely audible over the wind. "Is this the Wilson place?"

"Do I know you?" Michelle peered up at him through her snow crusted lashes. He knew her name and whose ranch it was, so there was no sense standing out in the storm. "C'mon into the house. I need to get out of this wind."

Michelle opened the back door and shook the worst of the snow off before stepping into the blessed warmth of the mud room. The tall stranger followed her in. He slapped his Stetson on his thigh to knock off the crusted ice and snow and unwound the long scarf from his neck. Michelle turned from hanging up her wet jacket and took in the man's seal black hair and startling blue eyes. *I would definitely remember if I knew this guy.* Michelle licked her lower lip and ran her hand through her wet, tangled hair.

"Are you lost, or do you live around here?" Michelle queried him. *I wish!* She added silently.

"I just bought the Chetwynd place, over the coulee," he said, a smile warming his face.

"The Chetwynd place." Michelle paused, as the pieces fell into place. "You're the new vet?"

"Cale Benjamin." He stuck out his hand.

Michelle automatically shook the proffered hand. Her brain was in overdrive. *Damn Mary, she could have warned me he was gorgeous.*

"You're the fancy horse vet from up Calgary way." Michelle's voice sounded stern and disapproving even to her ears.

Cale's smile faltered a little, and a small frown creased his forehead. "I do some equine work up that way, yeah."

"I thought a guy like you would be living in the big city, not out here on the bald assed prairie. Not a lot of opportunity to make big bucks on ranch horses and cattle." Michelle couldn't seem to stop herself from being rude.

"I'm not a city guy." Cale grinned. "My parents ranch down near Nanton, so I'm used to the bald assed prairie."

"Huh." Michelle turned to the stove and set the kettle on the burner. "Want some tea or coffee? You must be cold." She remembered her manners at last, and her grandmother's voice

24

sounded in her inner ear. *Any folks is always welcome at this table, especially in a storm.*

"What about that dog you called Doc about. Where is she?" Cale hung his polar fleece under jacket on the back of a kitchen chair.

Michelle swung around from the stove, and her gaze immediately caught on Cale's hips, which filled out his jeans just the way they should. She swallowed hard and dragged her gaze back to his face. Cale's gaze burned into her, and Michelle lost any thought in her head except that she really wanted to feel his lean muscular body against her and to run her tongue over his sensuous lower lip. A deep smile creased Cale's face, and he cleared his throat, breaking the spell hanging in the air between them. Michelle shook her head and turned back to the stove, embarrassment heating her cheeks.

"She's in the front hall, by the door." Michelle indicated the door to the hall with her hand and lifted the whistling kettle off the burner.

She poured water into the teapot and covered it with a knitted cosy before following Cale into the darkened hall. She found him on his knees beside the dog. The pitiful thing was now mostly thawed out and emitting a decidedly toxic odour.

"Oh, my word, something must be rotting off for her to smell like that." Michelle knelt beside Cale and tried hard not to breathe in the sickly sweet stench.

The dog thumped its tail on the mat and licked Cale's hand as he slid his fingers under her chin to examine her head. His expert hands moved over the dog's body, all the while he talked soft nonsense to the dog. With a final pat on the animal's head, Cale sat back on his heels and looked at Michelle. An odd expression crossed his face before he looked away. Cale got to his feet and offered her a hand. Michelle ignored his outstretched hand and stood up quickly before taking a step back.

*What is wrong with me, for heaven's sake? He's no different than any other man around here. I want to touch him so badly, but I can't deal with the way he makes me feel. Damn Mary and her matchmaking, damn her all to hell!*

"Well, Mr. Hot Shot Vet, what's the verdict? Will she live?" She cringed inwardly at how harsh and rude she sounded.

"The paw on the injured leg is black and necrotic and will have to come off, the leg is smashed and dislocated, and in light of the damaged paw, I would say the whole limb should be amputated. The rest is cuts and bruises and starvation. The puppies are another matter altogether." Cale took a step back from Michelle, a puzzled frown creasing his forehead.

"I'll call Doc in the morning and arrange to take her into the clinic." Michelle flicked on the overhead light in the hall as she spoke.

*More light, that's what I need. It won't be so intimate with the lights on,* Michelle thought desperately.

Cale bent and scooped the dog up in his arms. He smiled at Michelle's startled face, turned, and marched down the hall to the kitchen. He gently set the dog in Rex's bed that was still by the woodstove and covered her with an old blanket from the pile on the spare chair.

"She needs a warm bath and something for the pain, before anything else." Cale rose and shrugged back into his coat. "I'll just step out to the truck and get what I need."

Michelle stared at the back of his broad shoulders as he walked into the mud room, she sat down abruptly onto a kitchen chair and let out the breath she hadn't realized she was holding.

"What is wrong with me?" she muttered. "What is it about this guy that has me tied up in knots?"

She was still sitting at the table with her chin propped on her hand when Cale returned with his medical bag. Snow clung to his black wavy hair and sparkled on his thick lashes. Michelle tore her gaze away from his face and pushed away from the table.

"What do you need?" she asked, glad to have something to keep her hands busy.

"Is there a place we can bath her down here, or is the bathroom upstairs?" Cale set the medical bag on a chair and shed his coat.

"There's a shower down here." Michelle opened a door off the kitchen and turned on the light.

27

Cale gathered the dog in his arms and shouldered his way past Michelle as she held the door open for him. He set the dog down on the floor of the shower stall and took the hand held shower head Michelle reached down for him. She adjusted the water temperature to lukewarm and then knelt beside Cale to hold the dog while he applied the stream of water.

The shower room was small and only meant for one person. Michelle's hip was pressed firmly against Cale, and he had to reach across her to clean the dog's face. Michelle rested her chin on his shoulder because there was no room to do anything else. Her heart kicked into double time, and she hoped fervently Cale couldn't hear it. The dog sat quietly on her haunches while the vet shampooed her belly, careful of her swollen teats. With her long coat slicked back by the water and the mud taken out of it, the swollen bulge of the dog's pregnancy was strangely at odds with the rest of her. The dog turned her head and rested her chin on Michelle's wrist. As if she was too tired to hold her own head up anymore.

Cale washed the last of the frozen mud and ice from the dog and applied shampoo again. The dog slid down onto the floor of the shower, her injured leg thrust out to the side awkwardly. Michelle held her head up with one hand and gently helped Cale clean the injured leg with her other. Twice his fingers brushed hers, and it was all Michelle could do not to snatch her hand away. She gritted her teeth and mentally chastised herself. *Stop it for God's sake! He's a vet, and you hardly know him. Stop it!*

The memories flooded back, unbidden and unwelcome. The smell of shampoo and the warm hiss of the water confined in the little shower stall took her back to a place in her mind she avoided like the plague. Memories of Rob's hands on her body, slippery with soap, his fingers in her hair; his lips everywhere. Both of them tired from long days in the saddle, sometimes full of weary exhilaration if it was a winning day at the rodeo, and Rob had day money in his pocket. Michelle dragged her thoughts away from dangerous territory and tried to focus on the dog under her hands. *And look how that turned out, you idiot. He took off for the big city at the first chance he got.*

"I think that's as good as she gets." Cale's voice rumbled in her ear and broke the stream of memories.

Startled, Michelle jumped and tipped over against him. Her head came up quickly, and she was caught in the snare of his electric blue eyes. She watched, mesmerized as a small frown creased his face, and then he lowered his lips to hers, stealing the breath from her. Cale's lips were warm and sensuous, thrusting Rob's memory out of her mind. Electricity shot through her body as he explored her mouth. His tongue licked her lower lip before he caught it gently in his teeth. Sensation flooded her, and lights burst behind her closed eyelids. Cale buried a hand in her silky hair, trailed kisses down her jaw and breathed against her ear before delicately running his tongue along her earlobe. Michelle pressed against him, overcome with the need to be closer still. There were no coherent thoughts in her head, only sensation and the knowledge she wanted to be close to this man forever.

A flurry of water splattered Michelle's face. She pulled back from Cale's embrace and scrambled to her feet. Cale remained on his knees by the dog, now upright and preparing to shake the water out of her wet coat a second time. A fire burned in his blue eyes, and a smile crossed his damnably kissable lips.

"I think she wants a towel." Suppressed laughter made Cale's voice throaty and sent shivers of desire up Michelle's spine.

"I'll get some," Michelle managed to croak as she fled into the kitchen.

She grabbed four thick towels out of the laundry room and halted in the middle of the kitchen with the towels pressed to her chest. Her heart beat at triple time, and she felt light headed. *Okay, so he's gorgeous, and he can kiss like nobody's business. That's all it is, simple lust, nothing else. What in God's name was I thinking?* Michelle took a shaky breath and crossed the floor to the shower room door. She thrust the towels through the opening, being careful to not let her fingers touch Cale's as he took them from her.

"I'll fix a bed up for her," Michelle turned back to the relative safety of the kitchen and fussed with Rex's bed.

Cale carried the damp dog to the bed and laid her down. Michelle placed water and some soft food nearby. The dog took a token lap of the water and then drifted off to sleep in exhaustion. Her injured leg looked worse now it was clean, and the damage was easier to see. The frost bitten paw was already starting to slough flesh. Cale put a loose dressing on it and administered another dose of pain meds.

He stood and grinned at Michelle, who refused to meet his gaze. His shirt clung to his body, wet from the shower the dog had given them both. Michelle realized in the same moment her own shirt was soaked as well, and the top button had somehow pulled free of the flannel and was gaping open. Heat rose up her neck as she realized what Cale was grinning at, and she re-buttoned the shirt with clumsy fingers.

"I'm going to change into something dry, and I'll find you something of George's to wear." Michelle almost ran from the room.

"Who's George?" Cale's voice followed her out into the hall.

Michelle didn't bother to answer him and took the stairs two at a time. She reached the safety of her bedroom and leaned against the closed door. Her breath still came fast, and her heart skipped in her chest. Quickly, she stripped her wet clothes off and changed into jeans and a thick sweater. The wind whipped against the house, cold fingers of air curling through the window frames of the old house. The upper hall was freezing when she crossed it and entered George's room. Michelle scrounged around until she found some jeans and a flannel shirt in his chest of drawers.

Hugging the clothes to her like a shield, Michelle padded down the stairs, her thick socks making no sound as she reached the front hall and continued into the kitchen. She stopped inside the door just as Cale rose from where he was kneeling by the black dog. He gave her a brilliant, heart stopping smile as he caught sight of her.

"Those for me?" Cale eyed the armful of clothes with a hopeful expression.

"You can change in the other bathroom." Michelle pointed to a door beside the wood stove.

He crossed the room and took the bundle of clothes from her arms, managing to let his fingers trail down her forearm as he stepped away.

"You never told me who George is," Cale said casually, his eyes intent on her face.

"My brother." Michelle was irritated at the breathless catch in her voice.

"Oh, well, good then." Cale grinned and headed for the bathroom door.

Michelle told herself not to watch as the vet's cute behind sashayed across her kitchen, but then she gave up and just enjoyed the sight.

She turned back to the table and picked up the monitor. The mare and foal seemed happy and content. The colt had his head stuck under his mother's flank slurping up a second dinner. The foal finished eating, and the mare turned to pick at her hay. The afterbirth was still tied to her tail and swung heavily against her hocks. Michelle checked the clock and mentally calculated the time since the mare foaled. With a sigh she acknowledged the mare should have passed the afterbirth by now. She grimaced at the wet snow stuck to the kitchen window and the sound of the wind howling in the eaves. She picked up the heavy sweater from the back of the chair and pulled it over her head. Winding a scarf over her head, she tucked the ends into the front of the sweater.

"You're not going out again in this?" Cale's voice startled her as he came out of the bathroom.

Michelle swung around quickly and then burst out laughing. George's jeans were a size too small, and the sleeves of the flannel shirt ended above Cale's wrist bones. For a split second, Michelle wondered when wrist bones had gotten to be so sexy before she pulled her mind back to the matters at hand.

"The mare hasn't passed the placenta yet, and it's way past time." Michelle moved into the mud room as she spoke.

"Good thing the local vet is here," Cale joked while reaching for his own jacket.

"You don't have to come out," Michelle began.

"I went to school so you horse people could pay me the big bucks. C'mon, Michelle, don't stand in the way of my road to riches." Cale's eyes twinkled with suppressed laughter.

Michelle's face turned beet red, and she made a production out of pulling her boots on. *Damn, the man! He must have been in the UFA the other day... That's exactly what I said about him to Gary.* Michelle was acutely aware of the vet's presence behind her as she stepped out into the force of the blizzard.

Cale followed her, his treatment bag bumping the back of her thigh. He reached out and caught Michelle's arm with his free hand.

"Hang on to me, so we don't get separated in this. You know your way around this place like the back of your hand, but I don't," Cale shouted over the wind.

Michelle nodded and placed her mittened hand in Cale's larger one. A strange warmth ran through her, and she didn't stop to think about why she felt so safe, she just enjoyed the sensation of her hand firmly engulfed in his.

The wind and snow buffeted them, and Michelle was happy to have the larger body of the vet to shield her from the worst of the storm. It took both of them to get the barn door open with the snow drifted up against it.

Michelle flicked the switch by the door, and light flooded the interior of the barn. Pulling off her snow encrusted mittens she stuffed them in the big pockets of her coat. The buckskin mare whickered softly at the sound of voices. She held out her hand and smiled as the big lips searched her palm for a treat. Cale came to lean on the door beside her.

"Nice little fellow." He smiled at the spindly legged foal who blinked up at him through long curly lashes.

The buckskin mare turned her large liquid eyes on him and snuffled the collar of his shirt as she inspected him. Deciding the stranger was no threat she dropped her head and lipped some hay from the floor of the stall.

Cale set his bag on the floor and opened it. Michelle watched as he filled a syringe from the small bottle of oxytocin he selected from his bag. He straightened and smiled at Michelle. She returned the smile before she remembered she didn't like the fancy city boy vet. She stood back and let Cale hook the halter from the front of the stall in his large hand and open the door to the stall. Her eyes narrowed as she watched the buckskin mare's reaction to a stranger near her newborn foal. A smile played about her mouth as she remembered Doc vaulting over the stall door after Hot Shot's first foal was born, with the mare in hot pursuit, her teeth bared.

*Good thing Doc was still pretty spry six years ago.* Michelle chuckled silently at the memory.

Cale walked confidently up to the mare's shoulder, and she lowered her head for him to slip the halter over her ears. Michelle grudgingly scored one for the vet. The mare rolled her eye toward the foal but followed him over to the door.

"Hold her head will you?" Cale said without looking at Michelle.

She took the cotton shank from his hand being careful not to let her fingers touch his. Cale located the vein in the groove of the mare's neck and slid the needle through the skin. He pulled back on the plunger of the syringe, and Michelle heard his small grunt of approval as bright red blood bloomed in the colorless liquid. Michelle scored him another point for being careful and making sure the needle was set correctly in the vein. She watched as he administered the drug, stopping halfway through to pull back on the plunger again and ensure the needle was still seated in the vein. He removed the needle with an easy practiced skill and capped it before placing it in the sharps container in his bag. Michelle removed the halter from the mare and searched the straw for signs of the colt's manure. Locating the small heap of dark dung, she smiled in relief and followed Cale out of the stall.

She leaned on the door and watched the horse while Cale closed his bag. Sweat darkened the golden coat as the oxytocin took effect. The large muscles in the mare's abdomen clenched in the drug induced contractions. Her concentration on the mare was so complete she didn't take notice of the increasing force of the storm as it hit the barn.

Ten minutes passed before, with a final heave, the mare expelled the afterbirth into the deep straw. Michelle quickly slipped in and wrestled the heavy, slippery membrane out into the aisle in front of the stall. Quickly, she spread the large membranes out on the floor and was relieved to see both the horns were there and intact, nothing was left inside the mare.

"Cale," she began and then stopped. The aisle behind her was empty, and she frowned. *Where in God's name did he go?* She left the membrane on the floor and headed for the tack and feed room. Michelle pulled the door open and was relieved to see Cale talking on the wall phone. Michelle rarely used the thing, it was only for emergencies, or when her cell phone couldn't get a signal. She turned and left the room without speaking and returned to the birth caul in the aisle.

She gathered the edge of the membrane and rolled it toward the centre. It was cold and sticky, and before long her fingers were numb. Stubbornly, Michelle persevered until it was a somewhat manageable bundle. She squatted over it and began to put it into a large black garbage bag. The placenta resisted her. As quickly as she poked part of it into the bag, another part slipped back out. Her cold hands wouldn't co-operate, and the heavy bundle slipped away from her. Michelle lost her balance and sat down hard on the aisle of the barn.

"Jesus fucking Christ," Michelle muttered in exasperation. "Where the hell are you George, when I need you?"

Michelle blinked back tears of frustration. Her butt hurt, she was cold and tired, and there was still the damn dog in the kitchen to tend to. Cale's hand entered her blurred vision, and she placed her hand in his and allowed him to pull her to her feet.

"Afterbirth won, did it?" His smile warmed his eyes and his voice.

"You could say that, Einstein." Michelle refused to be cajoled.

"C'mon, Michelle, I didn't laugh." Cale's eyes crinkled in amusement. "Well not out loud anyway," he amended. "For a pretty girl you sure can cuss. Mary didn't warn about that." A mischievous grin creased his face.

Embarrassment crept its crimson way up her neck and flushed her cheeks. Michelle changed the subject quickly.

"Who were you calling?" she asked tersely. "Have to cancel a hot date with a big city girl?"

"Actually, I was talking to my mom. She worries when it storms, and she knows I'm out in it. No confidence in me at all; assumes I'm shiny side down in a ditch somewhere." Cale shook his head at the folly of mothers everywhere.

"Your mom," Michelle said incredulously. "Is it storming in Calgary, too?"

"My parents ranch south of here, near Nanton." Puzzlement coloured his voice. "I told you that in the house. What made you think they lived in Calgary?"

"I don't know where I heard that." Michelle refused to meet his eyes. There was no way she was going to admit to listening and participating in the speculative gossip in town.

Cale scooped up the messy afterbirth and dumped it into the empty wheelbarrow outside the tack room. She sighed and decided to leave dealing with it til the morning. Michelle trailed along behind him chewing furiously on her lower lip. Damn the rat bastard, not one bit of gossip mentioned he was actually from a ranching family. All she had heard was he was some hotshot horse vet who pandered to the rich and elite show jumping and dressage world. Lost in her thoughts Michelle walked smack into Cale's chest as he stepped out of the tack room after washing the sticky blood and amniotic fluid off his hands. His arms came up and held her steady while she regained her balance. Michelle braced her hands on the front of his jacket and involuntarily raised her eyes to meet his. Her breath caught in her throat and fire spread through her. Cale gazed into her face for a moment and then set her firmly on her feet away from him.

"I'm going to check on that mare, and then we should get back to the house while we still can." Cale left Michelle standing mutely by the tack room and strode to the buckskin mare's stall.

"Get a grip, woman," Michelle muttered under her breath.

She followed Cale to the mare's stall and was relieved to see all was well. She picked up five flakes of hay from the bale outside the stall door and tossed them into the manger. Michelle checked to make sure the waterer wasn't frozen and double checked the latch on the door.

"That should do her 'til tomorrow, even if the storm gets worse overnight." Michelle allowed herself a small smile.

"Back into the storm, then?" Cale buttoned his coat as he spoke.

Michelle nodded and flicked off the aisle lights as Cale wrestled the door open in the biting wind. She ducked under his arm, waiting while he closed the door and secured it against the wind and snow. Michelle didn't protest when Cale took her hand and set off toward the house. Checking her bearings, she was happy to note Cale was indeed headed in the right direction. They paused to catch their breath in the lee of the garage and then plunged the last few metres to the steps of the porch.

Two feet of snow had drifted unto the porch while they were in the barn. Michelle was happy enough to let Cale plow a path through it and walked in his footsteps. Her legs were like lead, and her teeth were beginning to chatter. Once inside out of the wind, Michelle leaned her back against the door and unwound the snow encrusted scarf from her head. She set her wet gloves on the washing machine lid to dry and shook the worst of the snow from her coat. Running cold fingers through her wet hair, she led the way into the bright warmth of the kitchen.

The black dog still slept by the woodstove. Michelle knelt down and ran a gentle hand over the dog's rough coat. The electric lights flickered and died as she stood up.

"Is there a flashlight anywhere?" Cale's voice came disembodied out of the sudden darkness.

"There's one right here." Michelle found the right drawer by instinct and flicked on the flashlight. "I'll light the oil lamp in a second."

She followed the pool of light spilling from the flashlight in her hand and located the matches where she set them on the table earlier. The sharp smell of sulphur stung her nose as the match flared into life, and she held the small flame to the wick of the oil lamp. A soft yellow glow filled the kitchen with intimate shadows and gave it an insulated, homey feel. Michelle took the flashlight and collected another oil lamp and some afghans and pillows from the living room. She paused for a long moment and studied the large space cleared for the Christmas tree she still had to drag into the house. She dismissed the thought with a sigh and headed back to the kitchen to take care of the matters at hand.

"Looks like you're spending the night," Michelle said a little too brightly as she entered the kitchen.

"I can make it home. It's only across the coulee." Cale reached for his coat. "The truck has plenty of road clearance. I should be able to plow through the drifts."

"You go then, cowboy." Michelle pointed her chin towards the door. "I bet you don't get out the laneway."

"You're on, lady." Cale took up the challenge. "The mighty Dodge hasn't let me down yet."

Michelle didn't bother to respond but set the afghans and pillows on a big stuffed chair by the woodstove. She crossed the room to peer out the window through the driving snow. A small smile played on her lips. The drifts were enormous and, unless she missed her guess, Cale's truck wasn't going anywhere in a hurry. The wind whipped the ends of the man's scarf wildly around his head as he entered Michelle's line of sight. The storm buffeted him backward a step for every two he took forward. She allowed herself a snort of laughter when Cale pointed his key fob in the direction he assumed his truck was and pressed the auto start. The lights of the truck were barely visible under the huge mound of snow engulfing it, the throaty roar of the diesel lost in the storm. Michelle giggled again, while Cale stopped and inspected the four feet of hard packed snow separating him from the truck door. Michelle scurried back to the table and poured the last of the lukewarm coffee into two mugs. A cold draft and a smattering of snow swirled across the floor when Cale came through the door from the mud room.

"Looks like I'm spending the night." He pointed his remote fob out the window and hit the kill button.

"The mighty Dodge, not so mighty." Michelle teased, forgetting she didn't like him, not one bit.

"The mighty Dodge is being held captive by a monster snow bank." Cale grinned at her.

"Snow banks are like that sometimes," Michelle agreed.

The dog whimpered in her sleep. Michelle went to her and stroked her head. The animal's eyes flickered open, and she curled her upper lip back from her teeth in a half-hearted snarl. Michelle spoke softly to her, muttering nonsense, knowing it was the sound and intonation of her voice that mattered more than the actual words. The dog heaved a sigh which pulled her scruffy coat taut over her bones, each rib stood out in sharp relief in the lamp light. The mutt closed her eyes and drifted back to sleep, apparently deciding it was too much effort to bite Michelle's caressing hand.

"She's had a rough go, poor thing." Cale sat on his heels next to Michelle. "What are you going to do with her once the snow stops?"

"I'm not sure. I didn't plan on getting another dog until spring. It's so much easier to house train a puppy when the snow is gone." Michelle rose to her feet and looked down at the sleeping dog.

"I don't think she'll fare very well at the SPCA. She's not socialized, and she's in really poor shape. With that broken leg, they'll probably put her down. The fact she's ready to whelp isn't in her favour either." Cale looked up at Michelle through his thick lashes.

She ran her fingers through her hair and frowned. "I'll worry about the puppies when the time comes, I guess. She isn't going anywhere for a few days, except to Doc's for x-rays." In her heart, there was no question she would keep the dog. The poor thing needed a home, and besides, she still hadn't gotten around to replacing Rex.

The lamp lit kitchen was much too cozy for Michelle's liking. She was acutely aware of the man kneeling at her side. She turned away and picked up the bedding she left on the chair earlier. With quick efficiency, she made up two beds on the linoleum near the warmth of the stove. Sleeping anywhere other than the room with the woodstove was out of the question with the power out. A cold draft of air swept across the floor; Michelle looked up in time to see the vet's cute backend disappearing into the chilly mudroom. Her pulse quickened at the sight and a flood of heat coursed up her stomach, over her breasts, and into her face.

"Get a grip, girl," Michelle muttered. "This is the fancy horse vet. He's way out of your league."

Cale returned to the kitchen with some wood and put it in the wood box by the stove.

He dusted his hands off on his jeans and sank down onto the empty pallet beside Michelle's. Stretching out his long frame on the afghan he heaved a sigh of relief and relaxed.

"Might as well get some sleep. I'm done in from schlepping through all that snow."

His eyes closed almost before he finished speaking; in minutes his deep, slow breathing told Michelle he had actually fallen asleep.

She watched the slow rise and fall of his chest. Her gaze travelled upward to his face, soft and vulnerable as he slept. Her hand moved by its own accord, and she had to restrain herself from stroking his cheek. With a muttered curse, Michelle jumped up and made herself busy turning down the wicks of the lamps and checking the fire. She returned to her makeshift bed and lay down with her back to the sleeping vet. No matter how hard she tried, she couldn't get comfortable, and her heightened senses relayed every tiny noise he made to her tired brain. Finally, she fell into a fitful slumber until an exhausted sigh woke her to find the dog crawling under her blanket. Michelle put an arm around the presence next to her, who in her dreams wore the face of the man who slept behind her.

Chapter Three


Michelle woke to the rumbling of a deep male voice. She rolled over and blearily focussed on Cale sitting cross-legged on his pile of blankets and conferring with someone on his cell phone. He smiled at her as she untangled herself from the dog and the blankets that had gotten wrapped around her during the night. She gave him a quick nod in return, quickly folded her bedding and placed them along with the pillow on the washing machine in the little laundry room off the kitchen. Without waiting for Cale to finish his conversation, Michelle pulled on her coat and boots and headed out to the barn to check on the buckskin mare and her foal.

The snow must have stopped sometime in the early hours of the morning, and the sun shone in a blue Alberta sky. The light bounced off the white surface and made it hard to judge the depth of the drifted snow. Michelle was covered in snow from getting mired in drifts by the time she made it to the barn. The horses whickered in greeting at the sound of the door sliding open. The buckskin and her baby were doing just fine, and Michelle made short work of her chores. She checked on the state of the round bale of hay that fed the small herd of horses outside. It was half buried in snow, but she could see where the animals had dug it away. One of them lifted his head out of the bale and regarded her with snow all over his muzzle and a big clump of hay perched between his ears hanging down into his eyes. Michelle chuckled and began her trek back to the house. It was easier going as she followed the trail she made earlier.

The throaty sound of a big diesel engine broke the pristine silence of the morning. Michelle stopped as Cale came into sight, moving snow with the big John Deere. He waved when he saw her but didn't pause. Good thing the man had the sense to find the equipment shed and fire up the tractor. Michelle shrugged and continued to the house. One less thing for her to worry about. The power was back on, so Michelle set about making breakfast. Cale had folded his bedding and placed it with hers in the laundry room. The pancakes were ready and sitting on the warming plate while Michelle finished frying the sizzling sausages. Her head came up in surprise as Cale's blue Dodge diesel drove by the kitchen window. He raised his hand in farewell and carried on up the narrow path he cleared with the tractor. Michelle watched in disbelief while his tailgate disappeared in the rooster tail of snow the big four by four kicked up. She turned off the burner on the stove with more force than was necessary and picked up the plate of pancakes. She dumped two onto her plate and frowned at the remaining flapjacks as if it was their fault there was no one to eat them.

"Well, dog, it looks like you hit pay dirt this morning."

The dog thumped her tail on the floor, and a thin string of drool hung from her mouth. Michelle placed the plate on the floor, and the dog started to eat with one eye on Michelle. She must be hungrier than she was scared this morning and willing to risk a beating in order to fill her stomach.

"Silly dog, no one's going to hurt you anymore." Michelle spoke softly to the emaciated animal.

She spent the next three quarters of an hour digging her truck out and left it idling to warm up while she figured out how to get the dog out of the house and into the passenger side of the vehicle. The dog took matters into her own paws and limped across the kitchen when Michelle came in the door. She followed Michelle out onto the porch and with the stoic courage only an animal can muster, walked on three legs through the snow to the truck. As gently as she could manage, Michelle lifted the dog up onto the passenger seat before going around getting in the driver's side. The black dog laid down on the seat, her head resting on the saddle blanket. Her eyes followed every movement Michelle made. The truck nosed through the snow which had blown into Cale's tracks from earlier in the morning.

"Men are just a big pain in the ass, dog." Michelle complained as she turned onto the gravel road at the end of her lane. At least the county snow plow had been by at some point.

The dog responded with a deep sigh and licked Michelle's hand. Once they reached the paved road, driving conditions improved, and before long, Michelle pulled up in front of Doc's office. She smiled at Mary when she pulled the curtain aside to see who was at the clinic this early in the morning. By the time Michelle opened the passenger side door and had the dog in her arms, Mary was holding the clinic door open for her.

"Go into the exam room on your right, dear." Mary said as Michelle wrestled her way through the door. The dog was skinny as all get out, but she was a big dog, and she wasn't too sure going into the vet's was such a great idea.

"Sit, you silly thing." Michelle admonished the dog as she heaved her onto the exam table.

"My stars, where did you find her?" Mary ran a gentle hand over the dog's rough coat.

"Under the front porch, in the middle of the storm." She leaned on the table to catch her breath.

"The poor thing's starved half to death, and her poor leg." Mary's voice softened with sympathy. "What's her name? I'll need it for her records?"

"Name?" Michelle looked blank. "Damned if I know. Probably doesn't have one judging from her condition."

"You want I should just write down Michelle's Black Dog?" Mary smiled, the lines around her bright green eyes crinkling.

"I don't know, Mary." Michelle threw her hand up in exasperation. "Call her Storm."

"Storm it is, then." Mary bustled back out to the reception desk to create a file for the new patient.

"Storm, who is going to cost me a small fortune," Michelle muttered, but she stroked the dog's head comfortingly.

"Did Cale make it out there last night?" Mary stuck her head back in the door, an expectant look on her face.

Michelle ground her teeth and forced herself not to snap at one of her oldest friends. "He did actually."

"And…" Mary prodded. "Did he make it home in that storm?"

Michelle counted mentally to ten before she answered. "No, his truck got snowed in. He left this morning."

"He seemed awful pleased about something when he stopped in here earlier," Mary volunteered.

"Not from anything I said or did." Michelle forced herself not to blush. The news the fancy horse vet spent the night at her ranch would be all over town before you could say "nothing happened." The door snicked shut behind Mary, and Michelle could hear her dialling the phone. No doubt calling her best friend and crony, Gerty.

"Hey, Michelle." Doc entered the exam room by the door from the kennels and the operating theatre for the small animal part of his practice. "Who's this then?' He extended his hand toward the dog who curled her upper lip back from her teeth.

"Some stray that wandered in during the storm, looks like someone beat on her, or she got hit by a car."

"Hmmm, let's see then, little dog." Doc talked softly to the dog while he examined her.

The dog decided not to bite him, but watched his movements closely. Her body trembled, and her nails squeaked on the steel top of the table.

Doc stepped back and looked at Michelle over his glasses. "The leg's broken, needs surgery and maybe some pins. I won't know for sure until I take some x rays; then it will depend on what the rads reveal. I can excise the necrotic flesh on that paw and try and save the rest of the foot and leg. You sure you want to do this. Or should we just put her out of her misery?"

The dog, being no fool, chose that moment to turn her big eyes up to Michelle and lick her hand.

"She's pregnant, I can't bear the thought of killing puppies, too. Just do whatever it is she needs, and I'll scare up the money from somewhere. Your fancy horse vet thought it should be amputated; do you think you can save the leg?" Michelle heaved a defeated sigh. "I never should have let Mary make me name the damn thing."

"So you met Cale last night. What do you think of him, now you've seen him?" Doc scrutinized her face, looking for what, Michelle couldn't guess.

"I think he's an okay vet, took care of Liza and the foal last night. And the dog," she said grudgingly. "I still don't think he'll last around here, big money is with the hunters and jumpers, and the dressage queens." Michelle knew she was being unfair and stubborn, but damn it she was right.

"Have it your way, missy." Doc grinned at her. "I'll just get…what did you call her?"

"Storm"

"Storm, then, I'll just get Storm fixed up with some meloxicam for the pain and then take a look at the rads. Do you want to help, or should I get Mary to call you with the bad news?"

"I can help for a bit. George is still on the rig, so I have chores waiting for me." Michelle enjoyed working with Doc and tried to come in and assist him at least once or twice a week when he needed a pair of extra hands.

Two hours later, Michelle dropped into a chair in the small reception area and leaned her head back against the window. Mary came around her desk and sat down beside her.

"How's the dog?" Mary asked carefully, her expression wary.

"The dog is fine. I feel like I've been ridden hard and put away wet." Michelle frowned at Mary. "And don't take that the wrong way, I'm just tired. Winter is hard with George gone for twenty-eight days at a time. I wish his hitch was shorter, but the money keeps the ranch going right now."

"I have just the thing for you, dear. I bought a couple of tickets for a concert out at the East Longview Hall for tomorrow night. It's a new group, some local girls. They call themselves The Travelling Mabels. Do you good to have a night out. It's only a week 'til Christmas, you know." Mary went to her desk and rummaged around in the papers strewn across it.

"Christmas," Michelle groaned. "I still have to wrestle the stupid tree into the house. Crap, I forgot all about it 'til you mentioned Christmas."

"I knew the tickets were there somewhere." Mary plopped back down beside Michelle with a pink ticket in her hand. "Here, you take this, and I'll meet you there. Luke doesn't want to go. He's playing poker tomorrow night."

"Who are they? You said they were local?"

"You know the girls who sang at the steakhouse last fall a couple of times, Eva, Lana and Suzy? You have to come keep me company and drive me home in case Gerty has too much wine." Mary refused to let up until Michelle agreed.

"Fine, fine, I'll meet you at the hall, but you owe me a beer." Michelle got to her feet and headed for the door. "Doc says Storm can come home tomorrow, so I'll see you then."

"Bye, Michelle, drive careful." Mary said to the door as it closed behind Michelle.

Chapter Four

The next afternoon, Michelle settled Storm in the bed by stove and set food and water beside her. The thick bandages held the injured leg at an odd angle. The tip of her tail thumped the floor, and the dog licked Michelle's hand before she stood up.

"You be good, missy," Michelle told her. "I have chores to do before I meet Mary."

Michelle thanked her lucky stars the power was restored. She hated having to start the generator so the stock could have water. The damn thing never worked right for her; only George seemed to have the magic touch the generator required. It was buried under a snow drift at the moment anyway.

Two hours later, the chores were finished, and Michelle took a few minutes to lean on the buckskin's door and watch the long-legged baby cavort around the stall. She opened the stall and stepped onto the thick bedding of straw. The foal careened away from her and peered from behind his mom, his tiny horse face peeking out from under the mare's belly. The mare ignored her baby's antics and ambled over to Michelle looking for a horse cookie. Michelle fished in her jacket pocket and came up with a couple of krunchies which the horse lipped up gently from her hand. The foal came over on his spindly legs to investigate, being very brave now momma was there to protect him. Michelle held her hand out and let him sniff it. The foal's whiskery nose tickled the palm of her hand. She smiled when the colt took hold of her fingers and sucked them into his mouth.

"I've got nothing for you, little man. You need to talk to your momma about dinner."

Gently, Michelle disengaged her fingers and with a last stroke of the mare's neck, left the stall and latched the door. She ran a hand over her hair and picked out a few pieces of hay the wind had blown into it. Between the hay in her hair, the hay down her shirt and itching in her bra, she figured she could feed a horse 'til spring. She left the barn and headed back to the house to shower and change before heading out to the East Longview Hall. The ticket said the show started at seven. Michelle checked her watch and quickened her pace. The timepiece informed her it was a quarter to six, and she still needed to shower and get out to the hall. With any luck, the county should have all the roads cleared, at least enough for the four by four to navigate.

She hung her coat in the mud room and kicked her boots off by the door. Michelle stripped her clothes off and stepped into the shower. With the hot water sluicing over her body while she shampooed the hay out of her hair, Michelle suddenly remembered the last time she used this particular shower. Her hands stilled in her hair as Cale's face swam before her eyes. That stupid little smile thing he did when he was laughing at her; suddenly it felt like he was there in the shower with her. Michelle gave herself a mental shake and finished washing her hair. *What is wrong with me? I don't even like the guy.* Wrapping a big towel around herself, Michelle ran across the cold floor and up the stairs to her room. She pulled on a pair of jeans and a sweater with a Christmas design knitted into it. It was one of her favourites. Hand knit by her Gramma. She paused before grabbing some makeup and applying it quickly. Usually Michelle didn't bother with the stuff; but she reasoned, it was Christmas, and she should make the effort. Her shoulder length, dark blonde hair hung shiny around her face. The ends curling and refusing to lay flat. Michelle gave up on the attempt to tame the wayward tresses and ran the brush through her hair one last time. She pulled her good boots out of the closet and smiled as she always did when she thought about her dad. He used to call them her "Sunday go to meeting" boots.

Storm was sleeping contentedly in her bed, and Michelle made sure there was plenty of food and water as she crossed the kitchen. With any luck, the dog wouldn't use the kitchen floor as her bathroom before Michelle got back.

The clock on the dash showed 6:30 p.m. when Michelle started the truck. There was just about enough time to get there before it started. Twenty-five minutes later, she pulled the Chev into an empty spot in the yard which served as the parking lot. Her boots were loud on the wooden floor of the wide porch. When she pulled the door open and stepped into the warmth of the hall, she was relieved to see show hadn't started yet.

Michelle handed over her ticket and was surprised when Amy, who was playing hostess for the event, told her Mary paid extra for reserved front row seating. Michelle shrugged and figured Mary was being generous and helping support the girls in their new venture. The hall was crowded, and Michelle guessed it must be close to its capacity of two hundred. She edged her way toward the bar where she ordered a beer and took some jerky as well. Since she didn't allow time for supper, jerky would have to do. She gave up trying to find Mary in the crowd and set off to find her seat. Reserved seating. She smiled, usually at East Longview it was first come, first served. You had to get there early to get a seat near the front. Not that there was really a bad seat in the small hall, it was just a little homey western community hall. Fairy lights were strung along the edges of the ceiling and the modest stage at one end. There would be as many people leaning on the walls and watching as there would be sitting. The advantage to being by the wall meant a person didn't have to remove their hat so the people behind could see the stage. She grinned at the butterflies The Mabels had decorated the stage with.

Michelle made her way to the front of the hall and squinted in the dim light to see what number was on her ticket stub. The first two rows of chairs had masking tape on them with the numbers written in black felt pen. She frowned at her ticket and then checked the seat number again. There was only one seat open, and it did have her number on it. Mary was nowhere in sight. Michelle shrugged. The woman occupying the seat must be somebody visiting until the show started. Mary would show up from wherever she was and claim it shortly. The woman was probably gossiping with Gerty. She slid into the seat, stuck her beer between her knees, and fished in her pocket for the jerky.

The lights dimmed, and Amy stood in the spotlight, smiling out at the crowd, ready to introduce The Travelling Mabels. After a brief intro, the three women emerged out of the kitchen-come-dressing and staging room at the side and walked up the centre aisle of the hall. They appeared as black silhouettes from behind as they came out of the shadows toward the brightly lit stage. They arranged themselves on the stools. Lana was tall and swung her guitar across her lap. Sweeping the honey blonde hair behind her ear, she smiled at the crow. Suzy's dark hair glimmered in the stage lights as she settled her base guitar securely, her fingers stroking the strings. Eva was the front man and Suzy's mom. She cracked a few jokes before cueing the first song. Each lady was a talented musician in her own right, together they were magic. Michelle settled down to enjoy the concert, she noticed the chair beside her was vacant now and wondered where Mary had gotten to. Eva counted them in and the girls swung into the first number, their beautifully blended voices filling the hall. Someone slipped into the chair beside her, and Michelle turned her head to smile at Mary. The smile died on her lips, and she had to stop herself from gaping like an idiot. Cale's deep blue eyes locked with hers, and Michelle forgot how to breathe for a moment.

"Where's Mary?" she whispered.

"I could ask you that self-same question," he answered her quietly.

"Mary, damn you all to hell. I am going to kill you," Michelle muttered while dragging her gaze back to the stage.

The Mabels were in the middle of a rollicking song about a hound dog named Mabel. The lyrics made Michelle smile, and she almost forgot about killing Mary. She risked a quick peek at the man beside her. He seemed oblivious to her presence. He watched vivacious Suzy with an interest Michelle found disturbing. She dismissed him from her mind with some difficulty and focused on the music soaring to the rafters. When Lana sang the opening lines of "Alberta Blue", applause rippled through the audience. The number was one of Michelle's favourites from the gigs the girls played at the local steakhouse earlier in the year. The song captured perfectly the magic of the prairie and the mountains spread out to the horizon, while the sky burned blue above them. Michelle smiled; it was like touching magic. Unbidden, she turned her head to look at Cale, only to find him looking at her. Suddenly, Michelle was acutely aware of his thigh resting against hers and the heat of his shoulder and arm beside her. The sound of applause broke her trance, and she quickly turned away to hide the blush she could feel rising up her neck.

*Damn the man, and damn Mary. She is so going to pay for this.*

Michelle took the beer from between her knees and finished the last dregs before she set the bottle on the floor under her chair. The Mabels were swinging through the last song before the intermission, something about a guy in a bar who thought he was Elvis. Michelle was too aware of the man beside her to pay much attention. Relief rushed through her when the house lights came up, and Amy announced a twenty minute intermission.

Cale's hand on her arm stopped Michelle when she started to get to her feet and bolt for the bathroom. Anywhere away from Cale was a good place to be. She looked down at him and couldn't help smiling at the expression on his face.

"I didn't know you'd be here, Michelle. Mary told me she bought the tickets, but at the last minute, she couldn't go. It didn't make sense to let the ticket go to waste. Luke was supposed to be here, not you." His eyes pleaded with her to believe him and make nice.

"Trust Mary to work both ends against the middle." Michelle dropped back into her chair shaking her head.

"It is Christmas. Can't we just enjoy the evening and the music? Maybe forget the fact that for some reason you can't stand the sight of me." Cale entreated her.

Michelle had the grace to blush, before she offered him a smile.

"It is almost Christmas," she agreed. "Let's call a truce for the rest of the night."

"Why is it you don't like me, by the way?" Cale asked seriously. "People don't usually hate me on first sight."

Michelle was saved from answering by the fact the house lights dimmed, and The Mabels returned to the stage.

She enjoyed the rest of the concert, singing along to the ones she knew. Her voice blended richly with Cale's as the audience sang along to "Remember". Cale rested his arm across the back of her chair, and Michelle felt his fingers play with the ends of her hair. The hall seemed suddenly small and intimate, and she forgot why it was she didn't like the man.

Cale and Michelle filed out of the hall and stopped on the wide porch to admire the big prairie moon illuminating the snow-covered landscape. In the distance, the lights of nearby ranches showed in the darkness, but the moonlight and the prairie dominated the view from the hall. Michelle lingered, unwilling for the night to end. There were night chores to do though and the dog to check on. She stepped away from Cale with brief smile and turned as Cale followed her down the steps.

"Are you parked over here, too?" The moonlight made his face shadowed and mysterious as she tilted her head back to look up at him.

"Mary said you'd need a ride home," Cale explained. He waved his cell phone at her. "She just left me a message."

"I don't know why she'd think that, my truck is right..." Her voice tailed off as she raised her hand to indicate where she parked the Chev not three hours before. The snowy piece of prairie was empty; only tire tracks showed in the moonlight.

"Mary is going to die a slow painful death." Michelle ground the words out between her teeth.

"You mean she took your truck?" Cale said in disbelief.

"She surely did, but not before making sure you knew I would need a ride home." Michelle let the laughter bubbling in her chest sound in her voice. Mary knew she kept the spare key under the floor mat. Nobody locked their trucks at East Longview Hall.

"She set us up." Cale laughed, too. "Her and her cronies have been throwing all the pretty girls in the vicinity at me since I got here. I should have seen this coming."

"Me, too. Mary's been matchmaking for me ever since Rob ran off with his dressage queen and left me high and dry." Michelle mentally kicked herself, even as the words were leaving her lips. *What in God's name made me say that? I don't ever want to think about Rob and his princess again.*

"Rob was the boyfriend who done you wrong?" Cale guessed. "Mary said something about a fiancé and the situation not working out."

"Mary should mind her own business. It's ancient history. I need to get home; I think Storm is going to pop her babies tonight." She changed the subject quickly.

"The Mighty Dodge awaits, seeing as the Chev is AWOL." Cale swept his hat off his head and offered her a bow.

Michelle couldn't stop the giggle. "Fine, let's just get going, Romeo."

The truck was warm when she stepped up into the cab. Cale had the foresight to use his automatic starter while they were talking outside in the cold. The snow crunched under the tires when they turned out onto the road. The radio was tuned to the local country station, and they sang Christmas songs all the way home. They belted out "Six White Boomers" as they pulled up at Michelle's back door, and she smiled across the dark cab at Cale. His eyes seemed to darken as he leaned closer to her and raised a hand to her cheek. Michelle jumped back, and she fumbled with the door handle.

"I gotta go check on Storm," she said to the door, refusing to look at Cale.

"I'll come in and check on her leg. I told Luke I would to save him the trip out here." Cale opened his door and stepped out.

Michelle slid out of the truck and pressed her cold hands to her burning cheeks. She wished for the millionth time she didn't blush so easily. There was nothing for it, but to step away from the truck and lead the way to the door.

Storm thumped her tail on the floor in greeting when Michelle flicked on the light in the kitchen. The black dog nosed a still wet puppy toward her teats and then continued to lick the caul off the second puppy between her front paws. Michelle knelt beside the dog's head and offered her hand. Storm licked her palm and returned to her ministrations on the black puppy. Cale hunkered down beside her. The black dog spared him a glance before dismissing him as a threat to her and her puppies.

"Looks like she's taking care of things just fine," Cale remarked.

"So far; there's more than two in that belly." Michelle stroked the dog's still prominent back bone as she spoke.

Cale picked up the puppy between Storm's paws before he examined the bandages on her leg. Satisfied, he sat back on his heels and grinned at the two squirming puppies as they slurped up their first meal. He gaze turned serious when the dog's sides heaved in a contraction. He relaxed as another small creature emerged into the world. Michelle rose to her feet and got the makings for coffee from the shelf over the stove. Soon the invigorating smell of fresh coffee permeated the kitchen. Cale left the momma dog to her puppies and helped himself to a cup before he settled himself at the table across from her. Michelle slid the new Traveling Mabels CD she'd bought into the stereo and hit play. The CD jacket had butterflies all over it. She giggled when Eva's "Smolder Blues" poured from the speakers. *Now that I'm getting older, I gotta learn to smoulder. If I want some loving, and I might.* Cale grinned at her and raised a questioning eyebrow.

"This always makes me think of Mary. Can't you just see her and Doc smouldering away?" Michelle broke into uncontrollable giggles at the thought.

"That's not an image that's conducive to my love life." Cale joined her laughter.

"I don't have one for it to ruin."

"I don't believe that for a minute, Michelle." The laughter left his face.

"Believe it, Vet Man. I swore off men after Rob left."

"What did you call me?"

Startled, Michelle thought for a minute. What did she just say?

"Vet Man, I used to call Doc that when I was a kid. I can't for the life of me figure out why I said it just now."

"Does that mean you don't hate me quite as much?" Cale's voice softened.

"I guess it must be what it means." Michelle couldn't put her finger on exactly how she felt about Cale. Michelle broke the silence that settled between them. "Have you got your tree up yet? It's only two days 'til Christmas."

"I'm not putting one up this year. It's just me in that big old house, and I'm covering for Doc on Christmas day."

"Seems kinda sad. Carolyn always decorated the whole house weeks before Christmas..." There were too many memories, some happy, some not so much.

"How long did you know the Chetwynds?"

"All my life...us kids all grew up together. Rob and I were going to combine the two ranches once we got married."

"Rob was a Chetwynd? I bought his parents' place?" Cale's eyebrows rose in surprise.

"The only reason it was ever for sale is because his dressage queen wanted to be closer to Calgary. Rob would have been the third generation of Chetwynds to farm that land. His grandpa must be rolling in his grave."

"I'm sorry, Michelle. I didn't mean to make you uncomfortable." Cale laid his hand cautiously on hers.

"Over and done with. I don't wanna ride down that trail ever again." Michelle pushed back from the table and stood up. "Since you're not having a tree of your own, you can help me drag this sucker in and wrestle it into submission."

Michelle heard him set his mug on the table and follow her down the hall to the wood room by the front door. The air in the room was frosty and her breath hung in wispy wreaths. She reached between the snowy boughs of the tree and found the trunk with her fingers. Heaving the fir tree upright, she gave it a shake to knock some of the snow out of it. The evergreen towered over her head. Michelle sighed, she always did this, brought home a tree much bigger than what she really needed. It just didn't seem like Christmas unless the tree filled the big west window of the living room. The darn things always looked smaller outside. The only problem was going to be getting it through the door.

"Did you cut down a redwood, Michelle?" Cale's voice came from the other side of the bushy behemoth.

"It's a Douglas fir, smart ass."

"Will it fit through the door?" Cale didn't sound convinced.

"It came in, so it's gotta go out."

Michelle heard Cale grunt something unintelligible. She was pretty sure she didn't really want to know what he said.

"You ready? I'm gonna push from this side," she warned him.

She cocked the tree backward a bit so the stump end would go out first and heaved. The thick body of the fir went through the opening a lot easier than Michelle anticipated. The springy branches fluffed out again as soon as the bulk of the tree cleared the doorway. She heard Cale curse accompanied by a thump before the tree keeled over dragging Michelle with it. She landed on top of the bottom branches. Other than some fir needles in her hair and down her shirt, she was unscathed. Michelle raised her head. There was no sign of Cale.

"Hey, Vet Man, where are you?"

"Under your man-eating tree. Can you get off me?"

Michelle struggled out of the tree's embrace and stood on the bit of bare floor by the wood room doorway. The Douglas fir rolled and bucked with Cale's attempts to free himself. The air was practically blue with cuss words. Michelle stuck her knuckles in her mouth to keep from laughing out loud. He slithered out from under the tree and sat on his knees to catch his breath.

Michelle's gaze met his over the length of the tree, her face flushed with heat which owed nothing to her fight with the evergreen. Her laughter died, to be replaced with a tension that sent hot tingles of awareness through her body where they gathered in the pit of her belly.

Michelle couldn't look away from the dark fires burning in his eyes. It was a distinct relief when Cale broke the contact and stood up. He smiled at her before he bent to pick up the top of the tree.

"Do you want to try and stand it up, or just carry it this way?" His voice was muffled by the branches.

"We need to turn it so the butt end goes first, or all the branches will break." Michelle wasn't exactly sure how they were going accomplish that feat.

She stood back while Cale stood the tree upright and mentally blessed her grandfather for building the house with ten foot ceilings. Michelle moved toward the towering evergreen, thinking to help tip the top toward her. She jumped back when the fir seemed to shake itself and move down the hall toward the living room. Stifling her laughter, she followed in its aromatic wake. There was a brief pause while the tree and the doorway fought for supremacy. With much rustling and bending of branches, the fir won and slid through the opening.

"Where do you want this thing?" Cale's voice was strained.

"The stand is by the window. I'll get it."

Michelle retrieved the tree stand and looked at the green bulk in front of her. There was no way she could see to manage it, except get down under the tree and secure the stand while Cale lifted it and held the thing steady.

"Lift when I say." Michelle shimmied under the thick lower branches.

Without too much trouble, the stand was fastened, and Michelle crawled out from under the boughs. Cale offered her his hand, and she allowed him to pull her upright.

"You couldn't find a bigger tree?" Laughter danced in his dark eyes.

"It didn't look so big outside," she said defensively.

"It's nice though. My mom always gets a big tree. Every year she promises she'll get a smaller one next year, but she never does."

"I think it's beautiful. I love the smell in the house." Michelle smiled happily.

"Where are your decorations? You'll never get the topper on this monster without help." Cale eyed the green mountain blocking the window.

"The boxes are by the fireplace."

"How many do you have?" Cale looked at the pile of boxes in amazement.

"It's a big tree."

Michelle plunked herself down by the hearth where she began sorting and opening the boxes. She carefully unwrapped the crocheted ornaments her grandmother made, placing the starched crochet work nativity scene on the cleared space in the middle of the low pine coffee table. Before long, every surface in the room was draped with glittering garlands. Glass balls, along with a multitude of other decorations sat on every flat surface. With a shout of glee, Michelle emerged from the depths of a box with strings of lights clasped in her fists.

"Lights first, I presume?" Cale teased her.

"Of course, didn't your mother teach you anything?" Michelle shot him a look of fake annoyance.

"She taught me never to get between a woman with Christmas lights and her naked tree."

"Your mother is a smart woman."

The better part of an hour later, the tree glimmered with lights and sparkled with decorations. The only thing left to do was place the angel on top. Michelle stroked the soft folds of the topper's skirts, before caressing the feathers in her wings with trembling fingertips. Tears welled up in her eyes, and Michelle blinked rapidly to clear her vision. The angel had been on top of the Christmas tree every year for longer than she could remember. Gramma said Grandpa brought the angel home on their very first Christmas Eve as man and wife.

Michelle jumped at the sound of Cale clearing his throat. She shot him a watery smile, crossing the floor to hand him the shimmery ornament. She watched as he carefully held the angel while he climbed the step ladder that stood beside the fragrant evergreen. Michelle tried not to look at the entrancing sight of Cale's butt as the fabric of his jeans outlined the firm contours of his hind end with each rung he climbed. Michelle sighed in appreciation. The man could certainly fill out a pair of jeans.

She looked upward, past the enticing jean-clad butt, to find Cale grinning down at her.

Michelle felt her cheeks burn and knew they were fire engine red.

"I said does the angel look straight." Laughter danced in Cale's eyes, and Michelle cursed inwardly. Damn him for catching her looking.

"She looks great."

Michelle waited until Cale was on the bottom step of the ladder before exiting the room on the pretence of checking on Storm and the puppies. The kitchen seemed unnaturally bright after the intimate firelight of the living room. Storm happily nuzzled her feeding puppies with her nose. Michelle knelt beside her and counted six squirming puppies. She picked up a soft warm puppy and cuddled it to her chest. The little creature was black like its momma. Its tiny pink tongue stuck out of its mouth, and the small lips moved in suckling motions even in its sleep. Storm gave a huge sigh and stretched herself out flat on her side. She raised her head when Michelle returned the sleeping puppy to the bed with the rest of the litter. Michelle ran her hand gently over Storm's head before moving the two puppies lying on the dog's wounded leg.

"This is a little better than under the front porch, hmm, momma?"

Storm thumped her tail in agreement and settled her head on the padded rim of the dog bed, her back to the comforting warmth of the woodstove.

"How many did we end up with?" Cale's voice startled Michelle.

"There are six so far. I hope she's finished." Michelle stood up and turned to look at Cale.

He was standing with his hands thrust in the front pockets of his jeans, his hair mussed and looking very sexy after his fight with the monster tree. Her insides turned to mush when he grinned and felt the heat rise in her cheeks as she smiled back. Her heart gave a little dip when Cale slid his jacket on and set his hat over his unruly hair.

"I assume Mary will arrange to deliver your truck in the morning and get the gossip first hand?" Cale paused with his hand on the door of the mudroom.

"She'll be here bright and early. She better come bearing Tim Horton's coffee and breakfast muffins, or I'm not letting her in."

"I'll warn her to come armed if I see her at the office." Cale's voice faded as he closed the door behind him.

Michelle watched him cross the porch and jump down the two stairs into the deep snow. She stood at the window until his tail-lights disappeared down the lane. Out of habit, she walked into the front hall and waited to see the lights go in the Chetwynd's kitchen. No, not the Chetwynd's anymore. Cale's place now. Why did that feel so right? A light showed in an upstairs window, in what she knew used to be Mr. and Mrs. Chetwynd's room. A sigh escaped her lips. For the first time since Rob deserted her for his dressage queen, Michelle allowed herself to remember the wonderful times they shared growing up. The first time Rob kissed her was after a branding. She could almost smell the hot, dry aroma of dust, singed hair and cow manure hanging in the early evening air. Both of them tired, dirty, and smelly. Rob's hair reeked of smoke and sweat, his lips warm and alive on hers. She smiled. All her dreams and wishes came true in that one tiny moment in time.

Michelle shook her head, and noticed the light in Cale's room had gone out while she reminisced about things better left in the past. Where they belonged.

# Chapter Five

The shrill of the alarm cut through the dark December morning. Michelle rolled over and snuggled under the mound of quilts. She buried her face in the pillow and groaned at the sound of snow hitting her window and the soft music of the wind that found its way through the old window casings.

"I suppose it has to snow on Christmas Eve." Michelle threw back the blankets and scurried to the bathroom to let the hot water tap run while she rummaged for the makeup bag she just knew was in the back of the cupboard somewhere. In the three minutes it took for the hot water to finally make it all the way up to her bathroom, she found the elusive makeup bag and dumped it out on the tiny dry sink pressed into service as her vanity. The mascara she used before the concert was more dried up than it had been then, so she pitched it in the garbage can. She set the new eye shadows and foundation on the ledge by the mirror and hopped into the now steamy shower.

Michelle's thoughts wandered while she worked the shampoo through her hair. Last Christmas Eve, she and Rob were planning their wedding. The plans for the annual gathering at the Chetwynd's were all complete; even George was home last year.

"The past is the past, get over it," Michelle muttered sternly to herself.

Quickly, she finished her shower and dressed in work clothes before she ran down the stairs to check on Storm and the puppies. The black dog thumped her tail, giving Michelle the dog's version of a smile, but didn't disturb the sleeping puppies by getting up. The kettle was boiling as Michelle set a dish of food down by Storm's head and gave her a pat. She crossed the floor and took the kettle off the stove before it could whistle. The scrunching of tires on the snow outside brought a smile to her face. Mary parked Michelle's truck in its usual place and climbed out with two extra-large double doubles and a bag of breakfast muffins. Score a point for Cale; she grinned at the thought.

Mary breezed into the kitchen, set the peace offering on the table, and hugged Michelle.

"Merry Christmas, Munchkin." Mary used a pet name from Michelle's childhood.

"Merry Christmas, yourself. You should be a dead woman after the stunt you pulled last night, but seeing as you brought Tim's, I might just forgive you." Michelle opened her coffee and took a huge gulp before she sat down at the table and snagged a sausage and egg breakfast muffin from the bag. "Ah, nectar of the gods!" she enthused as the coffee aroma tickled her nose, before the warm liquid slid smoothly down her throat.

"Okay, give. What happened last night? Dr. Cale was looking mighty pleased about something this morning when he came into the surgery." Mary plunked herself down opposite Michelle and opened her own coffee.

Michelle regarded her with narrowed eyes just long enough to make Mary squirm. "I should tell you I walked home in the dark, or I got a ride with some slick city guy who tried to take advantage of me. I know you already weaseled it out of Cale and know he drove me home and checked on Storm, so I won't waste my breath."

"And…" Mary prodded. "What else, you can't keep an old lady hanging. It's not good for my heart."

"You don't have a heart, Mary." Michelle snorted. "If you did, you wouldn't have pulled that stunt last night."

"Oh, Chelly girl, it's time you let what happened with Rob go. I ran into his mom earlier this week. Rob and Kayla went to Vegas and got married last weekend," Mary said gently.

For a moment, Michelle thought she might pass out as all the blood seemed to leave her head and gather in a painful knot in her chest. Though on second thought, she might just hurl instead. With an effort, she forced her mouth into a smile.

"That didn't take him long, did it?"

"He really does love her, you know. " Mary held up her hand to stop Michelle when she opened her mouth to protest. "I watched you two grow up. You were high school

78

sweethearts; neither of you ever dated anyone else. Then, when Rob started following the rodeo full time, I watched you grow apart. He loved the road, and you wanted to stay home and have babies."

"He's not rodeoing now is he? He's hanging out with the dressage queen." The words burst out of her mouth with more venom than she intended.

"Well, Ella said that he wasn't giving up the rodeo, and Kayla didn't want him to. She was surprised at how they seemed to just fit together. It's so hard to think of one of you without the other." Mary swirled the coffee in her cup.

"It really doesn't matter if he married her or not, I guess. He wasn't coming back here any which way." Michelle's anger deflated in defeat. "I think I always knew I loved him more than he loved me."

"You're still coming to the house tonight, aren't you?" Mary changed the subject, much to Michelle's relief.

"Yes, it seems weird not to be going to the Chetwynd's though, doesn't it?"

"It does, but everyone from town is going to drop in at some point. The Sunday School kids are going carolling, and so are the 4H kids from the Horse Club. You're coming for dinner tomorrow, too. I won't take no for an answer."

Michelle laughed at Mary's fierce look. "I wouldn't miss your dressing and cranberry sauce for anything!" She reached for another breakfast muffin.

Storm lifted her head at the sound of the bag rattling. Michelle smiled at the entreaty in the dog's eyes. She knelt beside the black dog and offered her half the sandwich. Storm took it daintily in her teeth and dropped it between her front paws to inspect it. Finding it satisfactory, Storm swallowed it on one gulp. With a sigh, she settled her head back down and closed her eyes.

"Did you chew at all?" Michelle asked the dog.

"They never really get over the distrust, do they?" Mary's voice was sad.

"It's early days yet, but no they never do." Michelle agreed. "They think of food as bait and connect it with bad things happening to them."

"Cale was telling Doc her leg is worrisome. The antibiotics don't seem to be having the desired effect on the infection though her other wounds are coming along." Mary spoke softly.

"He checked her over last night, after we put up the tree."

"Cale helped you put up the tree?"

Michelle mentally kicked herself for supplying Mary with hot new gossip for her coffee clache. Well, the harm was done now, she supposed.

"Yup, I wasn't going to bother, but I had the damn thing in the wood shed, and he offered. It's no big deal."

"Umhmm."

Michelle didn't like the look in Mary's eye. That look usually meant she was planning something decidedly underhand. It was her "matchmaking" look.

"Come see the puppies," Michelle changed the subject.

Mary set her coffee on the table and crossed to the dog by the stove. Storm eyed her warily but relaxed when Michelle sat on the floor by her head.

"Oh, they're little darlin's aren't they?" Mary stroked a tiny black head with her index finger. "What are you plannin' to do with them all?"

"Haven't the faintest idea." Michelle shrugged. "Plenty of time to worry about that when they're weaned, I guess."

"What about her? You thinking on keeping her?

"Don't know. I don't think so. Maybe..."

"You need something to replace Rex, don't you?"

"We'll see." Michelle was uncommitted.

Mary straightened up and retrieved her coffee. "I gotta get back and spruce the place up for tonight and tomorrow. See ya later, dear" The woman was out the door before Michelle got to her feet.

She grinned as the truck spit snow from under its tires. Mary hijacked the ranch truck to take her back to town rather than wait for Michelle to drive her. No doubt she'd have Cale return it to her and then she'd be forced to give him a lift back to town. Mary's matchmaking never took a break. Damn, the woman was persistent.

* * * *

It was just gone five o'clock when Michelle climbed into her truck and turned the key. The engine growled into life. She smiled, drove out of the yard, and down the lane. The mound of packages piled on the seat teetered alarmingly but stayed in place. The first stars appeared, brilliant pin pricks of light in the ebony sky. A waning three-quarter moon hovered in the evening twilight, throwing a faint silvery glow over the snow-covered prairie. The country station was playing Christmas songs non-stop, so Michelle sang along with Dolly on "Hard Candy Christmas" as she drove into Longview.

Twenty minutes later, she pulled up in front of Mary and Doc's house, killed the engine, and silenced "Christmas in Dixie" in mid-chorus. Doc came down the steps as she stepped out of the cab. In minutes, he had all the gaily wrapped parcels in his arms, leaving Michelle to follow up the rear with her offerings of shortbread cookies and bread pudding.

The warm air in Mary's kitchen welcomed Michelle when she pushed through the door bearing her contribution to the potluck dinner. She deposited her dishes on the kitchen table before giving Mary a big hug. Doc came back into the kitchen after putting his load of presents under the tree in the big living room. He hugged Michelle and kissed her cheek.

"Merry Christmas, Chelly Belly."

"Merry Christmas, Vet Man."

Michelle laughed out loud at the look on Mary's face.

"You, two!" Mary scolded in mock exasperation. "I haven't heard you use those nicknames in ages. I thought you said you were too old to call Doc Vet Man anymore."

"It's Christmas, Mary!" Doc responded. "She can call me anything she wants, as long as it's not Late for Dinner. Come in by the tree and let me get you some wine."

Doc slung his arm around her shoulders and steered her into the living room. The atmosphere in the large room was bright with the sound of laughter, the tree sparkling in the alcove of the large bay window. Michelle accepted a glass of wine and smiled as Doc scurried off to answer Mary's summons from the kitchen.

Michelle visited with everyone; the warmth of friends and community spread over her in a comforting blanket. For the first time since Rob left, she felt at peace. Mary came out of the kitchen and settled herself at the piano whose shiny surface reflected the lights on the tree. Michelle drifted over to it, along with most of the guests in the room. The sound of Christmas carols rose in sweet harmony. Michelle blinked tears from her eyes as the memories of other Christmases surfaced in her thoughts. Gramma and Grandpa Pete, Dad and George—they had all celebrated here in this room over the years. She clamped the lid on her thoughts when Rob's face danced across her inner eye. Michelle turned her attention back to the carol Mary was playing and added her voice to the swelling chorus of "Angels We Have Heard On High".

A cool draft swirled through the room when the door in the kitchen opened and closed. Michelle glanced over her shoulder to smile a welcome to the newcomers. The smile died on her lips; her throat constricted painfully. Rob and Kayla stood in the archway from the kitchen leading into the living room. Michelle's lips moved with the words of the carol, but there wasn't enough air left in her lungs for any sound to come out. The heat of embarrassment and humiliation crept up her neck. Every eye in the room was fixed on her; she just knew it. She wrestled with her temper. She would *not* scratch those periwinkle blue eyes out of the girl's head. She would *not* remove certain parts of Rob's anatomy and serve up a special dish of prairie oysters for an appetizer. Michelle was determined to hide her feelings and behave like a grown-up. A faint spark of amusement flashed through her mind at the memory of her Gramma telling her to do just that. Except that time, Michelle was planning revenge on a fourteen-year-old Rob for dunking her in the water trough.

"Rob, Kayla, Merry Christmas." Michelle broke the deafening silence that descended as the carol singing trailed to an end.

"Merry Christmas, Michelle."

Ignoring the apologetic look on Rob's face, she stepped closer to Kayla and gave her a perfunctory peck on the cheek. Michelle barely heard Kayla's quiet reply through the sound of her pulse roaring in her ears. She needed to get out of the room, somewhere quiet. Idiot man, it was just like him to pull a stunt like this. Michelle picked up the empty chip bowl off the piano, gripping it like a life line. She smiled brightly, murmured something about refilling it and escaped to the kitchen. She braced both hands on the counter, the empty bowl sitting forgotten between them. *Breathe, just breathe.* Finally, the surreal feeling of disconnection faded. Now what to do? Every part of her rebelled at the thought of re-entering the cozy living room. Snatching her coat from the pile in the spare room off the kitchen Michelle bolted out the back door.

"Coward," she berated herself.

Nonetheless, she jammed the key into the ignition and reversed out of the driveway. The backend of her pickup slid sideways on the snowy road. Michelle eased off on the gas and straightened the truck out. She rolled her window down, the cold night air somehow soothing her anger. The tears came as her anger lessened. Michelle slammed her fist on the top of the steering wheel.

"Damn him, damn him all to hell!"

The lights of Longview disappeared from her rear view mirror before Michelle got control of her tears. She pulled over to the side of the road and laid her forehead on the steering wheel. A wintry breeze blew through the open window numbing the tip of her nose. With her tears dried and her anger fled, a heavy, empty feeling engulfed her. The reality of Rob and Kayla's marriage penetrated her heart. Her childhood dreams were over. The plans of merging the neighbouring ranches, following the rodeo circuit, having babies…gone, all of it gone.

"It's really over." Her voice came out dull and lifeless even to her own ears.

"What am I supposed to do now?" Michelle was adrift; her plans for the future all revolved around Rob and what he wanted. She always thought what Rob wanted was what she wanted, too. Now that she stopped to think about it, she wasn't so sure after all.

After wiping her nose one last time, Michelle put the truck in gear and drove at a more sedate pace back to the ranch.

\* \* \*

The warmth of the kitchen was heavenly. Michelle dropped her coat on the back of a chair and sank down beside Storm and her puppies. The black dog licked her hand and laid her muzzle on Michelle's knee, her deep brown eyes gazing adoringly up at her. Michelle stroked Storm's head for a moment before she reached over and placed one of the sleeping puppies in her lap. The little creature snuggled into a comfortable position and promptly went back to dreaming, her little paws twitching while her mouth made small suckling movements. *Lucky little puppy, you have no idea how different your life could have been.* She stroked Storm's head again and ran a hand over the dog's side to check how her ribs were filling in. "You know though, don't you, momma?" Michelle said softly to the dog who thumped her tail in agreement.

The clock in the hall chimed midnight. Christmas Eve was over. Christmas Day just begun.

"Merry Christmas."

Tears blurred Michelle's sight as she whispered the words out loud. Was this the harbinger of Christmases to come? Last year, they announced their engagement. This year Rob was married to his dressage queen, and she was alone. Michelle placed the puppy back with Storm and got to her feet. The blinking light on the answering machine informed her that a message was waiting. George's voice was loud and tinny in the quiet kitchen. Her brother wished her a Merry Christmas and promised to call on Christmas Day when his shift was over. She smiled thinking about telling him his mare foaled out and all was well. She supposed she should tell him about Storm and the new puppies, too. His hitch was up the day before New Year's Eve, so at least George would be around for New Year's Eve. Michelle jumped as the phone shrilled in the quiet kitchen.

"'Lo."

"Michelle, are you all right?" Mary's worried voice came through the receiver.

"Yeah, I'm fine, Mary. Sorry, I ran off without saying goodbye."

"I gave that boy a piece of my mind, I can tell you. Fancy him just showing up on Christmas Eve without warning anyone. He should have figured you'd be there. Sometimes that boy doesn't have the sense God gave a duck." Michelle could tell Mary was still on a tear about Rob and the stupidity of men in general.

"It's okay, Mary. In a weird way it was a good thing. I think I've finally accepted it's over. Really over. The Rob I thought I loved wouldn't have done that to me. Maybe I never really got to know the man he grew into, and I just kept on loving the boy who used to worship me."

Mary snorted in Michelle's ear, and she held the receiver away from her head for a moment.

"You're still coming for dinner tomorrow? Well, I guess it's today now isn't it?" Mary insisted.

"Yeah, I'll be in around eleven or so. Is it okay if I bring Storm and the pups? She gets lonely if I'm gone too long."

"Sure, bring 'em. Doc wants to check on the leg anyway. He was talking about her yesterday in the clinic."

"Thanks, Mary. I'm headed for bed now, or I'll never get up in the morning."

Michelle replaced the phone in its cradle with one hand and reached for the light switch with the other. The flash of headlights turning in from the road caught her eye through the window. She dropped her hand from the light switch and picked the phone back up. Michelle felt sheepish at her caution, but she wasn't expecting anyone, and she was alone out here. These days you just never knew who was coming down the drive, not like when she was a kid and never gave it a second thought.

"What the hell is he doing here at this hour?" Michelle said to Storm when she recognized Cale's truck. The dog thumped her tail, and then left her puppies to hobble over by Michelle, a growl starting low in her throat at the footsteps on the porch.

"Michelle?" Cale's voice was muffled by the door.

She flicked on the mudroom light and unlatched the door to let him in. Storm growled from the kitchen doorway. Cale stepped through the door and removed his hat. His hair fell forward over his forehead, and Michelle fought the impulse to reach out and push it back for him.

"What's wrong? Is there anything I can help with?" Michelle grasped for a reason for his visit. Only an emergency would bring him to her door this late on Christmas Eve.

"I saw your light on my way by and thought I would stop and say Merry Christmas."

"You didn't make it to Mary and Doc's tonight. Were you out on a call?" Curiosity got the better of her; she had to ask.

"No, I had some last minute things to take care of, though. There were no calls tonight, thank God." Cale sounded tired.

"Last minute shopper, huh?' she teased him.

"Something like that."

Michelle thought he sounded evasive. Her gut said he was leaving something out on purpose.

She watched while Cale bent down and extended his hand to Storm, who quit growling as soon as she recognized him. He stroked her head, running his hand over her ribs and down the bandaged leg.

"How's she doing with the puppies? Is she getting around okay?"

"She's managing fine. I'm worried about her leg though. I don't think it's healing like it should. Doc is going to take a look at it in the morning." Worry colored her voice.

"Doc's not on call. I am." Cale looked up at her through his thick silky lashes.

"I'm going in to spend the day with Doc and Mary, so Storm and the crew are coming for Christmas dinner, too." She smiled in spite of herself.

Storm jumped and barked at the sound of footsteps on the porch. Michelle swung around and reached for the latch. She heard Cale curse softly under his breath behind her.

"Cale, anybody there?" An unfamiliar female voice floated through the door.

"I told you to wait in the truck, Stacey. I'm coming in a minute." Cale's voice was rough with irritation as he got to his feet.

Michelle opened the door to find a dainty blue-eyed blonde angel on her porch. A blonde angel who fluttered her sugar plum lashes at Cale and laid her hand possessively on his arm. She turned and raised the wattage of her smile while she extended her hand to Michelle.

"I'm Stacey. Cale told me all about you and the poor dog. I want to see the puppies."

Stacey took a step toward the kitchen, stopping when Storm's growl rumbled a warning.

"The puppies are sleeping right now, and I should be, too." Michelle said shortly.

Stacey opened her pretty lips to disagree, but Cale took her shoulders and turned her toward the door.

"Later, Stacey. Go and wait in the truck, I'll be there in a minute." Cale exhaled sharply in exasperation as he gave her a little push toward the door.

"Don't be long then." Stacey pouted prettily before she exited the mudroom.

"Sorry, Michelle. Stacey is—" he began.

"You don't need to explain yourself to me. How you spend your time is none of my business." She cringed inwardly at the harshness of her voice.

"Michelle—" Cale tried again.

"Get going. Don't keep your girlfriend waiting, cowboy." Michelle forced herself to speak lightly and twisted her lips into what she hoped was a smile. "Go, git!"

"I'll see you tomorrow, then."

He seemed reluctant to leave the mudroom. Michelle just wanted him the hell out of there before she did something she would regret later. Cale closed the door behind him, his boots echoing hollowly on the boards of the porch. Michelle and Storm went back to the warm kitchen where Michelle switched off the light. She stood in the darkened window and watched the tail lights of the truck as Cale drove up the lane and turned toward his place. Silently, Michelle replaced the phone in the cradle and raised her hand to wipe away the tears slipping down her face. It was just too much in one night. Having Rob's marriage shoved in her face was bad enough, but no, Cale needed to come waltzing in with his pretty little blonde girlfriend.

"Why do I care if he has a girlfriend? I don't even like the man." Michelle sniffed to Storm. Storm wisely made no comment, but returned to her bed of puppies.

The massive Christmas tree in the living room mocked her as she passed the door on the way upstairs. Michelle detoured into the room and turned on the tree lights. The soft glow illuminated the empty room. She sank down on the scarred leather sofa which had sat in the same spot for generations. She stroked the soft surface, memories of other Christmas Eves crowding her thoughts. Loneliness gathered like a physical presence in her chest; Michelle couldn't remember ever feeling so alone. Her anchors were gone, Rob, her dad, her grandparents. She guessed she could include the mother she didn't remember. She pulled the knitted afghan off the back of the sofa and curled up under it, watching the twinkling lights on the tree. The tears were still wet on her cheeks when she eventually fell asleep.

# Chapter Six

Michelle pushed Storm's cold, wet nose out of her face before she opened her eyes. The black dog's tail thumped on the floor, her injured front leg poking oddly out in front of her. The pale light of the waning moon and stars filtered through the windows. Christmas morning had arrived, even if the sun wasn't up yet. Michelle threw off the afghan and swung her legs off the sofa. She ran her hand over Storm's head before she stood up and folded the knitted blanket. Storm hobbling behind her, Michelle went to the kitchen to get the coffee brewing and put a bowl of dog food on the floor. Pushing the away the lingering loneliness from the evening before, she headed out to do morning chores. After checking the waterers and feeding the buckskin mare and her foal, Michelle stepped into the dusty, warm chicken house. The hens were still sleeping and woke with a ruffling of feathers and contented chuckling.

"Morning, chicken girls." Michelle spoke softly while she rummaged under each warm brown breast for eggs. The hens regarded her with beady bright eyes before settling back into the straw nests. She placed the eggs in a large coffee can and securely latched the door before heading back to the house. Once the eggs were washed she snugged them into a cardboard carton. She put the carton on the table beside the Saskatoon berry biscuits ready to take to Doc and Mary's for Christmas morning breakfast. She took the time to shower and change her clothes before going to collect Storm and her babies.

"C'mon, Storm let's get those puppies packed up." Michelle knelt beside the puddle of sleeping puppies near the stove. She scooped them up one at a time and placed them in the kennel. Storm supervised the procedure carefully, placing her nose on each puppy as Michelle moved them from the bed to the carrier.

"You stay here and guard them while I put the rest of this stuff in the truck and warm it up." Michelle stroked Storm's head and kissed her on the nose before gathering up the items from the table.

Ten minutes later, Michelle drove down the lane, the truck's headlights cutting a swath through the pre-dawn darkness. The snowbound fields reflected the faint starlight, so the snow appeared to glow with a strange luminescence. Storm lay on the seat with her head on Michelle's thigh; the dog's injured leg stuck out, making it hard for Michelle to change gears.

"Merry Christmas, dog." Michelle spared Storm a glance before turning out onto the main road. The dog thumped her tail on the seat in response. The puppies slept in the kennel, oblivious to the hum of the tires on the asphalt.

The lights were burning brightly in Mary's kitchen when Michelle arrived at the door. Her arms were laden with puppies and contributions to Christmas breakfast. Storm hopped ahead of her through the door as Doc held it open for them.

"Morning, darlin'." Doc greeted her with a kiss on the cheek while he rescued the precariously balanced eggs from atop the pile in her arms.

"Merry Christmas."

"Michelle, I'm sorry that idiot boy decided to show up with no notice. Lord only knows what he was thinking." Mary bustled into the room, her hair pinned haphazardly on top of her head.

"He wasn't thinking, as usual. At least not about anything except what's important to him." Michelle hated the edge of bitterness she could hear in her voice.

"Young pup needs his ass skinned for that stunt." Doc growled.

"He is who he is." Michelle struggled to keep her voice light.

She grinned when Mary snorted loudly as she set bacon to sizzling in the huge fry pan on the stove. With the skill of long practice, Michelle moved to the counter and got the fixings for hotcakes, and before the bacon was done she had a stack of golden cakes in the warming oven. While Mary fussed with the bacon and added sausages to another pan, Michelle cracked eggs into a bowl. Doc set a cup of coffee by her workplace and squeezed her shoulder before he deposited another full cup by his wife.

"How many are we cooking for this year?" There could be anywhere from three to fifteen people for breakfast, depending on who Mary and Doc invited.

"Seven, I think." Mary didn't turn from the spitting bacon pan.

"Ten, you forgot Cale and his folks." Doc corrected her.

Michelle's hand stilled on the egg whisk. Her heart jumped into her throat, threatening to choke her before plummeting into her shoes. Damn and double damn. The only thing that could make the day more uncomfortable would be Rob and Kayla sitting there, too. She turned her suddenly hot face toward Doc.

"Who else is coming?" Silently she prayed he would not say those dreaded names.

"Ummm, you, me, Mary, Cale, his mom and dad, Lillie Carter, that little blonde friend of Cale's, and Rob, Kayla and Ella." Doc muttered the last three names, refusing to look her in the eye.

The whisk dropped into the eggs with a splash. She cursed under her breath while she fished it out. Merry freaking Christmas to me, she thought savagely. Cale and his little blonde, with Rob and Kayla thrown in for good measure. Michelle ground her teeth, whisking the yellow mixture into frothy frenzy. She tipped the contents of the bowl into the hot pan, stirring it with a little more vigour than was necessary.

"Am I going to have to break out the sutures and bandages before breakfast is over?" Doc's teasing tones soothed her flayed temper a bit.

"Not likely, I don't plan to give them the satisfaction." Michelle smiled at him over her shoulder while she continued to push the eggs around in the pan.

"That's my girl." Mary hugged her on the way to the fridge.

"You are in deep dodo, missy. First you throw me at Cale, and now you invite him and his girlfriend to Christmas breakfast. Not to mention my ex fiancé and his new wife. If it wasn't Christmas, I would have to do some serious damage." Michelle fixed Mary with a false glare.

"Saved by the bell." Doc interjected at the peal of the front door chimes.

"That's it, run you coward. Worried you might be next on the hit list?" Mary called after his retreating back.

"You and me are going to have a long talk later, Mary." Michelle promised.

Mary grinned at her unrepentantly and started to fill a platter with the rashers of bacon. Michelle joined her at the kitchen counter. Pulling the hotcakes from the warming oven, she accepted the bacon platter from Mary in her other hand before crossing the floor and using her backside to push open the dining room door.

She deposited the dishes on the maple sideboard and turned back to the kitchen to fetch the rest of the food.

Mary finished filling the coffee pot of her mother's silver service set and placed it beside the steaming tea pot on the sparkling tray. Michelle reached for the handles of the heavy tray and jumped back in shock when Cale's hand closed over hers. The solid warmth of his body against her backside was an unwelcome pleasure. She closed her eyes for a brief second to regain her equilibrium before she snatched her fingers away from the electric contact with his. She whirled around, meaning to put as much distance as possible between herself and Cale. Instead, she found herself caught in the circle of his arms, her face inches from his. She placed her hands on his chest to push him away. The minute her hands settled on the warm expanse of his upper body, she forgot that she meant to escape. His eyes captured her attention, and for the life of her, Michelle couldn't make herself look away. Abstractedly, she felt the buttons on his shirt pocket rise and fall beneath her fingers with each breath he took. The spice of his aftershave wove itself into her consciousness. She detected the faint underlying scent of iodine. She smiled in spite of herself. The smell conjured up happy memories of visits from Doc throughout her childhood. Someone coughed discretely behind Cale, breaking the spell he held over her. Quick as a flash, Michelle snatched her hands from his chest and ducked under his outstretched arms.

"You planning to stand there holding that tray, or are you taking it in for Mary?" Doc smiled at her and shut the door without entering.

Cale sought and held her gaze for a long moment before he turned and bore the tray out into the dining room.

It took Michelle a moment to catch her breath. She closed her eyes and offered up a silent prayer for the patience to get through the day. Releasing the breath she hadn't realized she was holding, her hands automatically picked up the last platter of food, and her feet carried her through the door into the dining room. Doc stood in the entryway gathering coats from the newcomers. Rob's gaze skittered by her, refusing to meet her eyes. Kayla offered up a tentative smile. Rob's mom, Ella, hurried across the floor and enveloped Michelle in a hug, careful of the full platter in her hands.

"Merry Christmas, sweetie."

"Merry Christmas," Michelle managed to mumble.

Placing the platter on the sideboard presented the perfect excuse to turn her back on the growing crowd in the living room. Frantically, she took a couple of deep breaths and willed back the tears of embarrassment and frustration welling in her eyes. Pasting a bright smile on her face, she turned and faced the others in the room. She ignored Cale who was trying to catch her attention, wiped her damp palms on her jeans, and gestured at the waiting table.

"Breakfast is ready."

"Let's eat." Doc was first to move toward the large table set with Mary's special Christmas china.

Michelle shovelled food into her mouth oblivious to the taste. This kind of stuff was supposed to happen in soap operas, not in her everyday life. If someone told her two weeks ago she'd be sharing Christmas breakfast with Rob and his new wife and the hot new vet who happened to have a cutesy blonde girlfriend, Michelle would have rolled on the floor with laughter. But no, here she was doing just that. Absently, she reached down and played with Storm's soft ears. The dog sat beside her, hoping for some bounty to hit the floor. Storm did not live by the ten second rule. Anything on the floor was fair game which she didn't hesitate to claim. The puppies slept soundly in the kitchen, safe in their kennel.

"Coffee?" Cale's voice startled her. The look on his face said it wasn't the first time he asked her if she wanted coffee.

"Sure." Michelle handed him her mug, forcing herself not to snatch her hand back when her fingers came into contact with his. Awareness sizzled through her; the intensity in Cale's gaze told her he felt it, too. Damn the man; he had one woman. She sure as hell wasn't going to be number two. Or even number one, if there was a number two.

Once everyone finished eating, they moved into the large living room. Michelle slipped out to the kitchen to check on the puppy brood with Storm and lingered over the dishes and washing up. The temperature in the room climbed a hundred degrees as Cale carried the last of the platters in from the table. He closed the door carefully behind him after depositing the china on the sideboard. His long legs brought him to the sink quicker than Michelle anticipated, and he caught her by surprise, taking a wet plate from her hand as she was setting it in the dish drainer. Her gaze flashed to his face, and suddenly Michelle forgot how to breathe. Dark fires of desire kindled in his eyes, bursting into raging flames as he set the plate down and settled his hands on her shoulders. Nothing existed except the heat in her belly and the expression on his face holding her mesmerized. Cale's head dipped toward her, his breath was sweet with the scent of coffee and maple syrup. What a silly thing to think was her last coherent thought before his lips captured hers. The dish cloth slipped through her fingers and splashed into the soapy water. She remembered how to breathe when Cale's tongue slid over her lower lip, Michelle clutched his shirt in her hand to keep from landing on the floor. With a fierceness that surprised her, she pulled him closer, catching his lip gently in her teeth. His heart hammered against her fingers fisted in the cloth of his shirt. Kissing Rob was never like this, never so overwhelming and blotting out everything around her. The thought skittered across her mind before fleeing at the touch of his hands in her hair. There was no room for anything beyond the feel of his body against hers.

"Oh, I'm sorry. Am I interrupting something?" Stacey's icy tones dropped heavily into the silence.

Michelle jumped in surprise and pushed away from Cale. He held her loosely in the circle of his arms, resting his forehead against hers for a moment. Michelle smiled slightly at the cuss words he whispered before he raised his head to look at Stacey.

"Nope, not interrupting at all."

Cale shocked Michelle by pulling her into his chest and fastening his lips on hers. She stared at him in disbelief before her eyes fluttered close. Michelle felt Cale break the kiss and tuck her comfortably against him, his chin resting on the top of her head. Her pulse hammered in her ears; her brain refused to process any thoughts.

"What just happened?"

"I think I just kissed you." Cale's chest vibrated under her cheek.

"Why?" She couldn't think of a nicer way to phrase her bewilderment.

"Why does any man kiss a woman?"

Cale drew back from her, so he could see her face. Michelle lowered her head; she didn't want him to see the emotions she was sure were plainly written on her countenance.

"Look at me, Michelle. Stop running away from me." He commanded gently.

The sound of the door opening startled her, and she pushed free of Cale's embrace.

"Mary's looking for you, Chelly." Rob frowned as he quickly interpreted exactly what it was he interrupted.

"Don't you ever call me that again." Michelle flashed angrily at Rob as she pushed by him to get out the door. She turned in the doorway, fixing him with a cold stare that surprised even her at the intensity. "Never. We're not kids anymore, and I'm not sure I even know you now." Before Rob could get a word in, she spun on her heel and marched through the door, which snicked closed behind her with a prophetic finality.

Michelle found Mary by the Christmas tree, waiting on her before they started to open the pile of gifts glittering under the green branches. Cale and Rob joined them minutes later, laughing at some shared amusement. Michelle threw them both a dark scowl sure their merriment had something to do with her. Men, cowboys always sticking together, at the moment the sight of both men sickened her. She turned when Mary laid a hand on her arm.

"This is from Doc and me. I hope you like it." Mary handed her a gaily wrapped package and kissed her cheek.

Michelle peeled the paper back from the box and dug through the tissue paper inside. Her fingers found the treasure, and she pulled it from the wrappings. The morning light fell on the framed painting she held in trembling hands. The oils brought the subject to life—Michelle and Tags, her barrel horse, in full flight rounding the third barrel and heading for home at the CFR in Edmonton the year before. Tears sprang unbidden to her eyes and spilled down her cheeks.

"It's amazing. Thank you. How did you know I wanted something like this to remember him by?" Michelle leaned forward and hugged Mary before she leaned back against Doc's knees and smiled up at him.

"I was there when you lost him, remember, Chelly? I know how much that horse meant to you." Doc laid a hand on her hair.

"I never should have put him on the trailer that night. I should have waited until the snow stopped in the morning." Rob spoke softly, and Kayla put her hand on his arm.

"It wasn't anybody's fault but mine. I could have made you wait, but I wanted to get home to tell everyone about..." Michelle's voice trailed off, she just couldn't force out the words. They were in a hurry to get home and tell everyone about the engagement. For a moment, bitterness flooded her mouth, regret curdled in her chest. What ifs didn't change anything. Couldn't take back the semi-truck with a pup trailer jack-knifing into Rob's truck and trailer. Didn't change the fact Tags was crushed in the trailer. Michelle closed her eyes against the memory of him screaming. Horses should never have cause to scream like that, ever. The only good thing about the night was Doc following them and being there to slide the needle into his vein and stop the pain. Michelle remembered crawling into the mangled wreck to hold him steady while Doc wriggled in to end it. The snow swirled through the wreck of the trailer, the wind howled wildly, driving wickedly across the highway. Tags quieted when he heard her voice and felt her hand on his head. Then he was gone, the light stealing from his eyes as she watched.

"Chelly, don't think about the bad part. This is supposed to remind you about the good times and what a great team you were." Mary wiped tears from her eyes.

"I know." Michelle sniffed and rubbed the tears from her face with her shirt sleeve. She scrambled to her feet, clutching the painting and started for the kitchen. Rob and Cale moved forward to follow her.

"I need a minute alone. I'll be right back." She hurried through the door, fresh tears streaming from her eyes.

Storm stuck her nose into Michelle's hand when she sat down at the table, staring through blurred eyes at the painting. Suddenly, it was all too much. Rob and Kayla, Cale and Stacey, and what the hell was he doing kissing her in the kitchen when his girlfriend was in the next room? What the hell was *she* doing letting him kiss her in the first place. Thank God Cale's parents weren't able to make it for breakfast.

Meeting them would have more than she could take right now. Without stopping to analyse why, she scooped up the puppies, tucked them in the kennel, and headed out the door with Storm on her heels and the painting snugged under her arm. She fished the keys out of her pocket and within seconds had everything inside. She turned the key, waited impatiently for the glow plug, and started the truck. She reversed out of the drive, glancing back at the house before slipping the truck into first gear and driving onto the snow-packed road. From the corner of her eye, she saw Cale, or maybe Rob, coming down the back steps. Michelle turned her gaze resolutely to the narrow road in front of her. She checked her rear view mirror before pulling out on to the highway, breathing a sigh of relief when it remained empty. The last thing she needed right now was to talk to anyone.

Snow spiralled down from the cloudy sky. She grinned at the capriciousness of the Alberta weather. An hour ago, the sky was blue and the sun shining; now it was clouded up and snowing to beat the band. She stroked Storm's head where it lay on her thigh. Shortly, she turned down her lane and parked by the porch in the lee of the garage.

"Well, pretty dog ,what are you and I going to have for Christmas dinner? You think I should have thought about that before we bolted?"

Storm followed her out of the truck and stood with her tail wagging while Michelle gathered up the kennel and her painting. The black dog hopped up the broad steps and waited by the door.

Once inside, Michelle stirred up the fire in the kitchen stove and then rummaged in her pantry for a suitable Christmas dinner. The phone rang sharply in the stillness of the empty house, startling her into dropping a tinned ham on the floor.

"Oh, for the love of God, just leave me alone." She raged at no one in particular as she crossed the floor.

"Hello?" Michelle growled into the phone.

"It's me, Michelle. Are you okay? I just wanted to make sure you got home okay." Mary's tone was soothing.

"I'm fine. I'm home."

"We're sorry, honey. We both thought the painting was the perfect gift." Mary sounded on the verge of tears.

"I love the painting, Mary." Michelle let out a deep breath. "It's just….just everything. You know, Rob and Kayla, Stacey. Cale. It's just too much for me today. I mean last year I was all excited about getting married, and now…well, now Rob's married but not to me, and I've got the ranch to run by myself. I just couldn't stay, Mary. Please tell Doc how much I love the picture. I'll run in tomorrow, and we'll have tea and a visit. I've gotta go, Mary. Love you."

"Love you too, girl. Call me if you need anything. You have something there for dinner, or should I have Doc run out with a care package of turkey and stuffing?" Mary offered.

"I fine, Mary. Really, I just need to be alone."

Michelle hung up the phone and dropped into a chair by the table. She supported her head on her hands and stared out the window at the swirling snow. A glance at her watch told her it was going on three in the afternoon. She shook her head and stood up reaching for the cup on the table. The curdled cream floating on top of the cold coffee made her grimace. She carried it over to the sink and dumped the contents down the drain. Judging from the snow accumulated on the porch, Michelle had spent far too much time brooding over her cold coffee.

"Time for chores, little dog." Michelle set a bowl of food down for Storm, laughing as the puppies wriggled their way toward it. "You're too young yet, puppies; let your momma eat."

Michelle made short work of the chores, and she stepped out of the shelter of the barn, pulling the door closed behind her. She automatically checked to be sure the latch was caught and turned to head toward the house. The short winter afternoon was deepening into twilight, the wind picking up and sending tall whirlwinds of snow spiralling into the darkening sky. What little light there was leaked out of the sky as she trudged through the deepening snow to the house. She paused on the porch when she spotted two points of light approaching through the blowing curtain of white. A smile crossed her face, trust Mary to send Doc out in a storm to bring her a Christmas care package of food. She felt the smile fade when the truck stopped by the garage. It wasn't Doc's truck. It looked like Cale's. Michelle ground her teeth and pulled the mud room door open with more force than was strictly necessary. She stepped inside and closed the door behind her. Leaning on it, Michelle used every cuss word she had ever heard. She stayed there in the dark room until boots thumped loudly on the porch. Michelle flicked on the overhead light before opening the door to Cale's knock.

"Mary asked me to drop this off to you." Cale stood in the open doorway; snow sparkled in his dark hair and adorned his wide shoulders. "Do you need any help with the stock? Doc was worried about you traipsing around the corrals on your own in the storm."

"Chores are done." Michelle said shortly, making no move to take the packages from his arms.

"Can I come in for a minute?"

Cale took a step forward, and Michelle reluctantly moved out of the doorway. She shut the door behind him before following into the kitchen. Mary would have her hide if she refused the care package of food.

A deep breath did nothing to lessen the tension in Michelle's chest. *Storm, you traitor.* A sense of betrayal lanced through her at the dog's display of happiness as she greeted Cale. The animal's long plumed tail walloped the floor while her tongue lolled out the side of the mutt's mouth. Cale set the food on the table before getting down on the floor to pet Storm and play with the puppies. Michelle stood stubbornly by the door, refusing to be drawn into the homey tableau playing out on her kitchen floor. Four puppies wormed their way into the vet's lap while another gnawed on his sock. She hardened her heart against the gentleness of his hands and the warmth of his smile when two puppies braced their sturdy legs on his chest and wiped his face with their tongues.

Tearing her gaze away from Cale and the puppies, she crossed the floor to the counter and started another pot of coffee. Watching the brew trickle into the pot made it easier for Michelle to stay mad. Watching the cute guy on her floor playing with puppies did nothing to fuel the fires of her anger. It was just too cute.

"Damn, you little rat puppy!"

Cale's exclamation brought Michelle's attention back to reality. She whirled around; coffee pot in one hand, cup in the other. Hot coffee splashed over her hand and onto the floor. She smothered an oath before setting pot and cup onto the counter. Turning on the cold water in the sink, she plunged her hand under the stream. Cale set the puppies back in their bed and scrambled to his feet. Michelle felt the bulk of his presence at her back even though she had no intention of looking at him. She started in surprise when he gently grasped her wrist, removing it from the cold water to take a look at the burn.

"It's nothing, just smarts a bit."

Michelle snatched her hand back and turned to glare at him. Laughter burst from her mouth instead. Blood trickled down the sides of Cale's nose from the tiny puncture wounds of the puppy's sharp teeth. A frown creased his forehead at the blood dripping onto his white shirt sleeve. Michelle picked up a clean dish towel from the counter and handed it to him. Cale wiped up the worst of the mess before applying a cold, wet towel to the wound.

"You forgot to mention the little beasts are part vampire."

"I don't recall you asking."

"Fair enough."

Cale grinned at her over the cloth held to his injured nose. Michelle reached up and pulled the cloth from his face, her fingers lingering on his. Involuntarily, she took a step closer when Cale tipped his head down toward her. The dish towel fell to the floor as Michelle closed her hands tightly on the fabric of his shirt. A shudder ran through her when Cale's arms tightened around her. For a moment, she forgot she was mad at him, forgot she didn't like him. Michelle's gaze was drawn to his mouth. She tipped her head back to see his eyes. The passion smouldering there jumpstarted her pulse. Her mouth opened, and she ran her tongue over suddenly dry lips. All the breath rushed from her lungs as Cale crushed her to his chest and captured her mouth with his. Shock held her immobile for a second, the next, she returned his kiss with a fervour that matched his. Michelle grabbed hold of her libido before it ran off with her. *The man has a girlfriend, you idiot.* Her sensible side spoke to the wanton part of her that was urging her to rip off his clothes. Forcing an elbow into his chest, Michelle broke free and scooted away from him.

"Isn't Stacey going to be annoyed waiting in the truck? I'm surprised she hasn't come knocking at the door looking for you." Michelle couldn't keep the tremor from her voice or stop the breathless hitch at the end of her sentence.

Emotion still darkened his gaze, tempered with a smidge of annoyance as Cale crossed the floor to grip her upper arms. Michelle stubbornly buried her hands in her pockets and stared at the buttons on his shirt. Briefly, she considered kicking him in the shins and locking herself in the bathroom until he left, or maybe kicking him somewhere a little higher than his shin. A tiny smile quirked the corners of her mouth before she could stop it.

"Whatever you're thinking, it doesn't bode well for me, I'm sure." His breath tickled her cheek. "Listen to me, Michelle. I'm not going to say it again. Stacey is not my girlfriend, understand, not my girlfriend. We went to high school together. She came to Longview to visit an old friend who just bought a house here.

She's had a rough go of it lately. Her fiancé cheated on her and emptied her bank account. She's my friend, nothing else."

"Didn't look like a friend to me," Michelle muttered obstinately.

"Stacey likes to tease. Sometimes what she finds amusing, I fail to appreciate."

Michelle wrapped her arms around herself when Cale dropped his hands from her shoulders and stepped back. Warily, she looked up at his face.

"You either believe me, or you don't. I'm done defending myself to you."

"I'm so confused, Cale. Rob and Kayla were the last thing I needed today. I thought I knew Rob and look where that landed me. We grew up together, for God's sake." Tears welled in her eyes.

"I'm not Rob. I will never be Rob. If you can't let him go, I'm wasting your time, and mine." Cale's words fell flatly into the space separating them.

Michelle tried to find the words to explain. Thoughts and phrases chased themselves around in her head, but she couldn't force anything to come out of her mouth. She watched numbly while Cale gathered his coat and hat before opening the mud room door. He paused and turned back to her. Michelle's heart jumped into her throat. The power of the joy his actions caused surprised her with its intensity.

"I forgot to tell you, George is home. He stopped at Doc's figuring you'd be there. I left him and Stacey with their heads together, yakking like long lost friends."

Cale jammed his hat on his head and yanked the porch door open. Quicker than a crippled dog should be able to move, Storm flashed across the kitchen through the open mud room door. She dashed between Cale's legs and disappeared into the blowing snow. Cale picked himself up from where he landed in the snow bank on the porch at the same moment Michelle arrived at the door in hot pursuit of Storm. She slammed into his chest and sent both of them back into the drift Cale just extricated himself from.

Spitting snow from her mouth, Michelle scrambled to her feet, ignoring Cale's grunt of discomfort as her knee dug into his ribs. Shielding her face from the biting snow, she searched the yard for Storm. Muttering a curse, she whirled toward the door, intending to grab her coat. Rough hands grabbed her, preventing another face wash in the snow bank. Cale set her down, glaring into her eyes for a second. Michelle could hear him muttering in the dark mud room. He emerged with two coats, handing hers over before shrugging into his own.

"I suppose we have to go find the damn mutt."

"I don't need your help. She's my dog, and I'll find her." Michelle let her temper sweep through her; who did the man think he was anyway?

"It's a blizzard for heaven's sake, woman! You can't go chasing around on your own."

"You're the one who let her out."

"Like I did it on purpose."

"Doesn't matter, does it? She's gone, and she's gimpy, and she's got puppies."

Michelle spat the words over her shoulder while she attempted to stomp down the steps. The heavy snow clung to her jeans, and she suppressed a giggle when she heard Cale slip on the stairs behind her. *Serves him right.* The thought warmed her even though she admitted it wasn't really fair to blame him.

Fifteen minutes of fighting through the snow and wind was all Michelle could manage. There was no sign of Storm, and no chance of finding her tracks on the windblown prairie snow. *Hell, I can't even see my tracks.* The feel of a hand on her shoulder was startling. Brushing the snow and frozen ends of her hair away from her face, Michelle shook her head at Cale.

"I can't hear you!"

Cale leaned closer. Michelle was very aware of the faint scent of his cologne and the hint of peppermint on his breath. "We need to go in. She'll come back."

Cold air whipped her face. It felt like the blood in her veins turned to ice. Reluctantly, Michelle nodded her agreement, and together they trudged toward the porch light which shone like a beacon through the icy storm.

116

Once back in the warm kitchen, Michelle paced from the door to the window and back. *Where is the damn dog?* Her jaw ached from clenching her teeth, and a headache pounded behind her eyes. Cale left off playing with the puppies by the stove to take his turn looking out the mudroom door. The sound of paws on the floor, and the tinkle of frozen snow in Storm's long coat brought Michelle racing to the kitchen door.

"What the hell have you got, dog?" Cale's voice was the first indication something was wrong.

Before she could ask for an explanation, the door pushed open, and Storm limped into the light. The dog was covered with ice and snow; the only black visible was her eyes. Storm dragged a huge snow encased thing in her mouth. The dog's eyes glowing with pride, she stumped to her puppies and spit the bird out in front of them.

"Where did she find a bird like that?" Cale nudged the carcass with his toe.

"Oh, my God! It's a peacock; damn it, dog." Michelle's hands flew to her mouth in dismay.

"A peacock?"

She nodded. "Old man Harvey on the other side of the coulee raises them for their feathers."

Michelle sank to the floor by the frozen bird and felt to see if the bird's neck was broken, or if it was still alive. No such luck, the thing was deader than a doornail. Cale knelt beside her and repeated the exam.

"Neck's broken."

"Do you think it could have frozen to death first?"

"Anything's possible, I suppose."

"Harvey's such a mean old coot. I hate to phone and tell him I have his dead bird on my kitchen floor."

"Maybe it got out somehow. I can't see how the dog could have gotten all the way over the coulee in this weather."

"I know I should tell him, but he'll want the dog shot. He hates dogs, threw a litter of puppies in the river a couple of years ago. It was only luck I was riding by at the same time. Poor little mutts." Michelle rested her hand on Storm's wet head, tears gathering behind her eyes.

Storm turned her adoring gaze on Michelle. *Look what I brought you, beloved human, food for my babies.* The big brown eyes were wide with pride and innocence. She knew the dog had no concept of the consequences of her actions. Storm was simply providing for her babies as best she could. The inevitability of what must happen now twisted Michelle's stomach into knots.

Closing her eyes helped to marshal her thoughts while the scenarios ran through her mind. Old man Harvey would throw a fit when she told him. He'd arrive to collect the dead bird for its feathers with his gun in hand. Tears slipped down her cheeks while her fingers continued to stroke the black dog's head.

"Couldn't you just offer to pay the guy for the bird?" Cale's voice was gentle.

Wordlessly Michelle shook her head. Old man Harvey wasn't known for his good nature or cooperation; the man was mean as cornered badger. *If only Cale wasn't here to see this, I could just make the damn thing disappear.* The vet was here though, and that was something she couldn't change.

In a swift movement, Cale lifted the heavy bird and carried it out the door into the snow. Michelle scrambled to follow him, grabbing her jacket from the hook. The flying snow hurt her face. Lowering her head, she plunged off the porch into Cale's tracks.

"Get back in the house!" His words were almost lost in the wail of the wind.

"What are you doing for God's sake?" Michelle clutched his arm in the lee of the truck.

"Go back in the house. You never saw this damn bird. Do you understand?"

Cale heaved the poor dead peacock into the bed of his truck before stepping into the cab and starting the engine. He met her startled gaze with a wicked smile and shut the door. The truck growled its way backward through the snowdrift before heading off up the lane. Michelle watched the progress for a moment before the cold and snow drove her back inside.

Collapsing on the floor beside Storm and her puppies, Michelle drew the dog's head unto her lap, stroking the rich black fur. *Where the hell is Cale going with that bird? No way he's taking it back to old man Harvey.* The thought he might do such a thing drove her to her feet. In minutes, any trace of the peacock's presence was obliterated from the kitchen. The driving blizzard would take care of any tracks, and in any case, the stupid bird had no business being out in the storm anyway. She snagged a towel from the pile of laundry and began to dry the melting snow and ice from the dog's coat.

Guilt niggled uncomfortably at her. Gramma would say she should phone Mr. Harvey immediately and offer compensation. er hand reached for the phone; she stopped unable to bear the thought of what would happen to Storm. Grandpa would say it was the damn fool's own fault if he couldn't look after his stock better than that. The sight of Storm nuzzling her puppies while protecting her bad leg settled the matter for Michelle. Turning from the phone, she started a new pot of coffee and sat at the table watching for the lights of Cale's truck.

An hour later, she saw lights come on in the house across the coulee. Seconds later, the phone rang sharply in the quiet kitchen.

"It's all taken care of. How's that dog with the broken leg doing?" Cale's voice was nonchalant although Michelle caught his unspoken message.

"She's fine, sleeping with her puppies. What have you been up to this evening?"

120

"Just out on a call, saw your lights on, and wanted to wish you a Merry Christmas. I'll drop by in the morning to take another look at the leg."

"See you in the morning."

Michelle replaced the phone in the holder, smiling in amusement. *What in heaven's name did that man do with the damn bird?* His cryptic message reminded her of playing cops and robbers as a child, making up nicknames and codes only her and George could figure out. Shrugging her shoulders, she turned out the lights and ran up the cold staircase to her room. A glance out her window showed the snow still swirling down. *Maybe George will stay in town tonight. I can't believe Cale said Stacey and George were all over each other. Surely my brother has more sense than that? Men! You never know what they'll do.*

Shivering, she slid into bed, pulling the flannel sheets up to her nose. Snuggling into the blankets, Michelle drifted into slumber, an amused smile on her face.

*What did Cale do with the damn peacock?*

# Chapter Seven

Dawn light peeked faintly in the window when Michelle woke up; the snow was drifting against the window panes but didn't seem to be falling anymore. Half asleep, she shuffled down the hall to the bathroom. Pushing through the half open door, she bumped smack into something.

"What the hell?"

"Oh, my God! What are you doing in my house?" Michelle's voice was sharp with annoyance and disbelief.

"George brought me." Stacey took a step back into the bathroom.

"Get out. Get out of my house now." The fist squeezing her heart made it hard to get the words out.

"My house too, sis." George's deep voice startled her.

"You brought her here?" Realization of the situation dawned on Michelle. "You slept with her? In this house?"

George laughed at her annoyance, reached around, and took Stacey by the hand. Pulling the pretty blonde to his side, he wrapped a long arm around her and steered her down the hall to his room.

"Got things to take care of, Chelly. We'll talk about it later."

Fury raged and seethed inside her. Slamming the bathroom door, Michelle regarded herself in the foggy mirror.

"Things to take care of my ass."

Finished in the bathroom, she strode down the hall and hammered on her brother's door. "Your turn to feed the stock, jackass." Stomping back to her room, she slammed that door, too, just for good measure. *He can do the chores today, I'm going back to bed for an hour or so.* The bed was still warm; gratefully her body melted back into the cocoon of blankets. Before she could remember to be furious with George, her eyes closed.

The glare of bright sun reflecting off new snow woke her three hours later.

\* \* \* \*

Studiously refusing to look down the hall toward her brother's room, Michelle stomped down the stairs as loudly as she could. A wicked amusement brought a grin to her face. George was a notoriously light sleeper. Sure enough, by the time the coffee was ready, George staggered into the kitchen walking very carefully, his eyes almost closed against the sunlight streaming in the window.

"Could you have made any more noise?" His voice came out raspy and low, but the set of his shoulders told her he was annoyed.

"Could you have found anyone else on the planet but *her* to warm your sheets?" Michelle let her own anger color her words.

"How the hell am I supposed to know you hate someone I don't even know you know?" George poured strong hot coffee into a mug and gingerly sat down at the table. "Does that even make sense?"

"You could have asked, you idiot. Doc would have told you, or Mary." She ground the words out between clenched teeth.

"Talk quieter for God's sake woman. It was Mary who introduced me to Stacey." George shook his head in bewilderment before realizing his mistake.

"Figures, the matchmaking queen meddling again. Although why that blonde wench I'll never know. Mary has some master plan in motion, but I'm not playing." Michelle wiped the already clean table with unnecessary vigour.

"Don't know, don't care. Going back upstairs." He muttered carrying his coffee out of the room.

"When is she leaving?" Michelle called after him.

"Yeah, we have to talk about that later." George hesitated in the hall just outside the entry.

"Talk about what? There's nothing to talk about except how soon you can have her city ass out of here."

"I kinda offered she could stay here until she gets settled." The big man ducked his head and waited for the assault.

"You did *what?* She leaves today. This is my home, and I'm not having that woman live here." Anger made her voice rise shrilly.

"It's my home, too. My money pays the bills." George closed his eyes wearily and leaned his head against the door frame.

"And who the hell do you think keeps the place running, busting my ass feeding stock and splitting wood while you're gone for weeks at a time? Not to mention foaling out your mare. Have you even gone and looked at the colt yet?" *This is not happening; he cannot be this stupid.* A sense of disbelief washed through her; she pinched her arm hoping to wake up from the nightmare. No such luck.

"Don't matter. Place is both of ours, and I asked her stay, so she stays as long as she wants. I looked at the mare last night, by the way." George turned and disappeared into the shadows in the hall. A moment later, she heard his feet on the stairs, and then the door to his room creaked.

"Stays as long as she wants, does she?"

The dish cloth landed in the laundry basket, its impetus aided by the violence with which it left her hand. Michelle stood rooted to the floor, so angry it was hard to think straight. *This is my home. There's no way I can share it with her, and what about when George goes back to work? Am I supposed to keep house for the blonde wench? Pigs will fly first.*

"George said there was coffee made, can I have some?"

Stacey's voice dragged Michelle's attention back to the present and away from murderous thoughts of what she would like to do to George, and Mary, too, for that matter.

"What?" She blinked stupidly at the blonde in the doorway. The woman managed to look beautiful even with an old bathrobe wrapped around her and no makeup.

"Coffee. George said there was coffee made." Stacey tucked a stray curl behind her ear and offered Michelle a small smile.

"On the counter." She turned and busied herself with Storm's puppies. *If I have to look at her much longer I'll be ripping her hair out.*

"Are those the puppies Cale told me about, the ones from the crippled mother?" Michelle started at the blonde's voice so close behind her.

"Yup." She refused to look up as the woman moved to stand beside her. Storm growled low in her throat, and her hackles lifted slightly.

"It's okay, silly dog. I'm not dangerous." Stacey moved to kneel beside Michelle.

Storm growled again and lunged to her feet, lips curled back over bared teeth.

"She doesn't trust people she doesn't know, and she has good reason." Michelle blocked the dog from reaching Stacey. "Get your coffee and leave."

Stacey straightened and moved toward the counter on the far side of the kitchen. Small tinges of guilt fingered through Michelle. Gramma's voice sounded in her head. *Anyone is welcome in this house, girl. Lessen you have a really good reason why they shouldn't be.* She didn't figure Gramma would see jealousy as a good reason for refusing the hospitality of the house. From the corner of her eye, she saw Stacey fill a mug with coffee and disappear down the hall. Breath escaped her lungs with a hiss as Michelle remembered to breathe. *Coffee, that's what I need. Coffee and a big stick to beat the pair of them with.* She had no sooner poured herself a mug and settled at the table to figure things out when the crunch of tires drew her gaze to the window. Cale waved and made his way to the door. A rush of cold air swept across the floor as he entered.

"What's up, Michelle? You look like you want to murder someone, and it can't be me. I only just got here." Cale grinned at her expression.

"Nothing's up, except Stacey is upstairs in my brother's bed."

"You're kidding me, right?" Cale ran his hand over his face.

"Not. She came home with him last night, and apparently, he told her she can live here for as long as she wants." She blinked sudden tears from her eyes. *Betraying rat brother, thinking with his other brain.*

"Huh, well it's good for Stacey, but I take it he didn't talk to you about it first."

"You think?" Frustration drove her to her feet. She stalked across the kitchen and filled a mug for Cale.

"Thanks." He took the mug from her hands. "Don't you want to know what I did with Storm's prize from last night?" Cale grinned wickedly at her from under the thick lock of hair which fell across his forehead.

"I am truly afraid to ask." A tiny grin niggled at the corners of her lips.

Cale sat in the chair beside her before speaking. "I took the thing over to Harvey's and left it in the ditch by the gate. There's nothing to tie Storm to it, no teeth marks or dog hair. It looks like it got smacked by a car, broken neck and a broken leg."

"Did anybody see you?" Hope came to life in her chest.

"There wasn't anyone out on the roads last night. The house is way down the lane, and the lights were out, so I think we're in the clear." The man grinned at her like a little kid who got away with swiping cookies from the jar.

"Why?" She didn't really care she supposed; the important thing was Storm's safety.

"Why what? Why would I engage in clandestine behaviour? I'm not a saint, Michelle. The dog wasn't gone long enough to get over there and back. She must have found it near here." Cale frowned at her. "Don't go all crazy on me and confess to the Harvey's, or I'll have a hard time explaining what I did."

"Thanks. For helping Storm and me, too." Michelle laid her hand over Cale's and squeezed his fingers.

"Our secret; don't even tell Doc, for God's sake." Cale's voice was laced with concern.

"Just you and me, promise." She removed her fingers from his hand.

"I like the sound of that, you and me." He smiled at her and slung an arm over her shoulders. "Truce?"

"Truce." She agreed. "Although it's pretty sneaky of you to use the old 'save the damsel in distress' situation to make me cave."

"Whatever it takes. Even if the damsel in question was a dog." He leaned his head against hers; the musk of his aftershave filled her senses.

"Are you going to Doc and Mary's for brunch?" Michelle broke away and stood up.

"Want a ride into town with me?" He waggled his eyebrows at her.

"Yeah, if you don't mind, I'd like that."

Cale carried his cup to the sink before pulling the kennel for the puppies out of the pantry. By the time Michelle washed up the few dishes, the puppies were in the kennel, and Storm was waiting by the door.

"All packed up and ready to roll."

Cale lugged the kennel out to his truck with Storm tailing him closely. Michelle turned off the coffee pot, dressed warmly, and joined Cale and the dogs in the truck. *George can make his own coffee when he drags his butt out of bed;*

*the dregs will be cold by that time.* The thought brought a smile to her lips.

The inside of the cab was warm and toasty. Cale settled the kennel of puppies on the back seat, and Storm scrambled onto the front seat. Michelle joined them, laughing when Storm called "Shotgun" in dog fashion by neatly walking over her lap and pushing Michelle toward the centre of the bench seat. With a huge sigh, the black dog leaned on the back of the seat and rested her chin on the edge of the window frame. Cale shot Michelle a look that started shivers in her stomach. She jumped when he stretched his arm across the seat behind her. Her breath came out in a tiny gasp as he removed his arm once the truck was backed out of the yard. She fought back a stab of disappointment and stroked Storm's head to hide her reaction. Her leg felt hot where it came in contact with Cale's thigh. She shifted away slightly, but the big dog on her right left little wriggle room. The sudden warmth of Cale's hand startled her as he twined his fingers with hers.

"Relax, I promise not to bite." The humour in his smile melted her resolve just a little, and she allowed herself to smile back at him.

There were a couple of other trucks in the yard when they pulled up to Doc and Mary's. Storm refused to move, so Michelle slid out the driver's side. She glanced into the bed of the truck, and her breath caught in her throat.

"Cale, there's a tail feather in the bed." She grabbed his arm and pulled him to the tailgate. "What are we gonna do with it?" Panic and hysterical laughter vied for control of her voice.

"Oh, for God's sake." Cale snagged the long peacock feather with his gloved hand. "Cover me." Throwing her a wicked grin over his shoulder, he made his way to Doc's burning barrel which was producing some feeble flames and smoke. Quickly he lifted the grate and folding the feather in two thrust it into the glowing embers.

"Is it gone?" Michelle peered past his broad shoulders as he returned to the truck.

"There's enough flame left; it's gone."

Suddenly, the absurdity of the situation struck Michelle, and she burst out laughing. Cale joined her, wiping his eyes with his gloved hands.

"It feels like when I was ten and putting something over on Grandpa," Michelle managed to get out between gasps of laughter.

Cale shook his head in agreement, still trying to catch his breath.

"What're you two caterwauling about out there?" Doc's voice cut across their shared mirth.

"Private joke, Doc. You had to be there." Michelle pushed away from the truck and grinned at Cale.

"Get your butts in here, I'm starving, and Mary won't let me eat without you." Doc managed to sound plaintive and put upon while amusement curled the edges of his words.

"Coming," they chorused together and gathered Storm and the puppies from the cab.

"The things I do for you, dog," Michelle whispered to Storm as she set the dog carefully on her three good legs.

"The things I do for both of you girls." Cale's breath was warm on her cheek as he reached into the cab for the kennel.

## Chapter Eight

Doc held the door open while Cale wrestled the kennel in, Michelle and Storm followed close behind. The dog settled in a heap under the table, the puppies crawling over their momma once the kennel was open. Cale and Michelle took the two empty chairs at the table.

"Thought I was gonna starve, girl. What took you so long?" Doc helped himself to the scrambled eggs and hash browns.

"It was kind of a weird morning. George gave himself quite the Christmas present," Michelle remarked dryly.

"What did that boy do this time?" Mary's eyes twinkled with supressed laughter.

"Like you don't know," Michelle accused her.

"Seriously, what did he do that has you so riled?"

"His new friend Stacey spent the night. I ran into her in the bathroom this morning."

"What's wrong with him offering her a place to stay for the night?" Doc spoke around his mouthful of pancakes.

"In his bed?" Michelle raised an eyebrow at him.

Doc choked on his pancake, and Cale helpfully smacked him on the back.

"He only just met the girl. I don't know what to make of young people today." Mary shook her head.

"You haven't heard the best part yet. George told her she can stay as long as she wants. I told him to take a long walk off a short pier."

"What did George say to that?" A frown creased Mary's forehead.

"Oh, it's all okay with him apparently. He ignored my opinion as usual. I think he expects me to babysit her when he goes back to work." Michelle stabbed a sausage with a little more force than was necessary.

"And you said…." Doc let his voice trail off.

"We didn't actually get to discuss it. He had more pressing matters in his room to attend to." She snorted.

"What are you gonna do? I can't see you going along with that scheme for too long." Clint, Doc's neighbor ventured to ask.

"I haven't figured that out yet, Clint. You don't have an extra room do you?"

"Land sakes girl, I can't have a pretty young thing like that staying with me. What would people say?" Clint's face reddened at the mere thought.

"I meant me, not her." Michelle glared at him.

"That's your home, Chelly. Don't be silly and let yourself get pushed out by a flash in the pan. You know how long George's relationships last." Mary scolded her.

"Mary's right; the girl will be gone by New Year's." Doc agreed.

"I wouldn't bet on that, Doc. Stacey can be pretty determined if she sets her mind to something."

Michelle felt Cale's gaze on her, but she refused to look at him.

"You think she's set her hat for George?" Clint leaned forward on his elbows eager for some gossip to share with his cronies at the hotel.

"Stacey's never been one to bed hop, so I'm guessing she likes him enough to hang around and see where things end up." Cale shrugged.

"She'll end up in the river pretty darn quick if she thinks I'm gonna be her personal maid and errand girl." Michelle growled.

"What's really eating you, Michelle?" Mary rested her hand on Michelle's arm. "C'mon and help me with the coffee."

Michelle waited until they reached the counter on the far side of the big room. "I don't know, Mary. I can't stand all the lovey dovey crap right now. First Rob and Kayla and now George and Cale's old girlfriend, right under my nose."

"Is this more about Rob, or more about the fact that she's Cale's ex?" Mary prodded gently over the gurgle of the coffee maker.

"That's just it, Mary, I don't know." Tears welled up in her eyes. "I'm kind of over Rob. I mean, I don't think I even know him anymore. It's like I was in love with who I thought he was and not the man he grew up to be."

"What about Cale? He certainly seems to be sniffing around a lot. Looks to me like he's pretty interested in more than that black dog of yours."

"I know, and I have feelings for him, too. I'm just scared, and I need time to figure it out. Without George and his lady love prancing around half dressed." She blinked the tears from her eyes. "Do you think Clint will rent me his spare room?"

"I don't think that's gonna fly." Mary laughed.

"I suppose you're right about that."

The coffee maker finished brewing with a loud burp. The two women quickly filled the mugs and brought them to the table. Conversation flowed around her barely noticed as Michelle drank her coffee. For the life of her, she couldn't figure out what it was about Stacey that bothered her so much. *Am I jealous?* She had to admit she was, if she were to be perfectly honest. *But why? I don't care who George dates. I just hate the fact she's so friendly with Cale.* A faint heat crept up her neck, growing hotter until her cheeks burned. *I can't be falling that hard for Cale. I don't want to be in love with anyone right now. Damn, damn, damn.* With an effort Michelle dragged her attention back to the conversation, ignoring the questioning look Cale shot her.

The men refilled their mugs and retired to the living room to continue their gossip. Mary and Michelle tidied the kitchen before settling back at the table to play their favorite game of cards.

Cale wandered into the kitchen a couple of hours later, interrupting the game which Michelle was losing badly.

"Oh, my stars! Look was time it is." Michelle pushed back from the table and looked at the tall man in the doorway.

"Yeah, I have to get back to the house and catch up on some paperwork. I didn't want to spoil your fun though."

"No fun really, Mary's scalping me as usual." Michelle laughed.

"Not my fault you can't bluff your way out of paper bag." Mary wagged her finger.

"Why don't you leave the puppies here for a bit?" Doc commented as he filled his coffee mug.

"I guess Storm could use a bit of a break. They're old enough to do without her for a couple of hours. The little heathens just finished eating."

"Clint's granddaughter might be interested in one or two, so this will give me a chance to show them off." Mary grinned.

"Okay then, you ready to roll, woman?' Cale handed Michelle her coat before he clipped a lead on Storm's collar.

"I'll take her." She held out her hand for the leash and led Storm toward the kitchen door.

The dog pulled back and whined in her throat, eyeing her puppies asleep in the kennel. Michelle gently guided her out the door and helped her into the truck. Cale followed, closing the door with a final wave to Doc.

"It's okay, dog, we'll come back and get the kids later." Cale ruffled the black dog's head affectionately.

# Chapter Nine

"Who left the damn gate open?" Michelle scrambled out of the truck before it actually stopped. The pen of first year heifers were scattered around the yard where most of them were taking advantage of the row of round bales. Several rolls of hay were pulled open and strewn about the snow covered ground. A red brockle-faced heifer raised her head and looked at the truck as the diesel rumbled into silence before returning to demolishing the hay bale.

"Are they all here?" Cale appeared beside her.

"I think so. There should be four black baldies, three red brockle-face, and two red white-face." She hoped her memory was correct.

Silently wishing Rex was still alive, Michelle spread her arms and walked toward the knot of heifers gathered at the nearest pile of feed. Four pairs of eyes regarded her, and then mooing softly, the heifers agreeably turned toward the open gate of their pen. She stepped back to allow three others through the opening as Cale herded them from behind. The remaining two obstinately refused to move from the far side of the round bales. Michelle came around behind to push them in the direction of their pen. Cale stood guard in the open space between the bales and the gate. The young cows rolled their eyes and shuffled through the snow in the general direction she intended. Reaching the open space, the lead animal bellowed loudly and swung her head, spraying the man blocking her way with snot. She lowered her head and charged with her accomplice in hot pursuit.

"Damn it all to hell! I'm gonna kill whoever didn't latch the gate. Bastard..." She gasped at the black baldy who charged Cale and knocked him flying into a drift. Her legs wouldn't move fast enough hampered as they were by the heavy snow. She floundered the last few feet in time to see the back end of the runaways disappear behind the chicken house. A snow covered figure emerged from the drift and shook itself, knocking snow everywhere. "Are you hurt?" She struggled not to giggle.

"Only my pride."

"Can you watch they don't get out of the yard? I'm going to drag George's ass out here to help."

The effort of stomping to the house and across the porch took some of the starch out of her anger. She banged into the kitchen without removing her outerwear.

"George, get yourself down here, and I mean now." Michelle bellowed and was rewarded by the sound of feet hitting the floor above here.

"What are you screaming about?" Buttoning his shirt, her brother came into the kitchen with a major case of bed head.

"Nothing except the pen of heifers are out." Sarcasm dripped from the words.

"Shit, did you get them back in?" He glanced out the window on his way to the mudroom.

"Except for two black baldies; they're over behind the chicken house. It's gonna take more than two people to get them corralled." Michelle waited impatiently while he pulled on boots and a coat.

"Sweetie, what going on?" Stacey stood in the doorway wrapped in quilt.

*Sweetie? Gag me with a fork.* Her brother was many things but sweet wasn't one of them. *Oh well, let the girl find that out for herself.* She pinned the petite blonde with her sharp gaze.

"Someone left the gate on the heifer pen unlatched."

"Which pen?" Stacey asked, her blue eyes wide and fixed anxiously on Michelle.

"The one nearest the chicken house."

"I closed it after George went through with the big bale," she said firmly.

"That's nice, but did you slide the chain through the latch?" Michelle wrenched the door open to see if Cale had managed to keep the cows cornered.

"What does it matter? Let's just get the stupid things back." George stamped past her out the door.

"Translated, that means you didn't latch the gate." She glared at Stacey. "Try not to help out again, will you?"

141

Slamming the door, she felt a little guilty. George was the one to be mad at. Grampa's rule was a good stockman always checked the gate, especially when working with someone who hadn't proven their worth yet. It was an unwritten, unbreakable rule. She reached the break in the row of bales and used her body to block the opening after pulling the pen gate open. George walked behind the chicken house, and the two escapees trotted out the other side. Cale encouraged them along with a cattle hook, and they scooted into the open gate. She hurried to close and latch it firmly behind them.

After throwing her brother a speaking look, Michelle turned her back and headed to Cale's truck. Storm sat in the passenger seat with her nose pressed against the window, covering the glass with dog drool and nose prints. She opened the door and helped the dog down. Storm hopped over to Cale and pushed her nose in his hand. Without hesitation, she limped to George and greeted him in the same manner.

"Don't be nice to me, dog. Michelle's pissed, and you might get the fallout." George's attempted humour failed to make her smile. She had outgrown the childhood ploy a long time ago.

"Do you want some coffee?" Ignoring her brother, she smiled at Cale and took Storm into the house.

The men followed her into the house. From the kitchen, she could hear them talking in the mud room but couldn't make out the words.

*Probably just as well.* She allowed herself a grin at the memory of Cale in the snow bank. Her amusement fled when Stacey entered the kitchen. At least the woman was dressed now. Feeling pigheaded, she allowed the blonde to stand uncertainly by the counter without acknowledging her. *It's a good thing Gramma isn't here. She would have tanned my hide for sure.* With the speed of long practice, she made a fresh pot of coffee and slapped four mugs on the table. Her contrary side prodded her to only fill three mugs and drive her point home to Stacey how unwelcome she was. *That is nasty, though, and she really hasn't done anything, except be stupid enough to sleep with George and believe his line of bull. If she wasn't so chummy with the vet, I could actually feel sorry for her.* She relented and filled the four mugs.

"Do you want to get the cream from the fridge?" She unbent enough to speak to Stacey.

The blonde smiled uncertainly but hastened to set the carton of cream on the table beside the sugar bowl. As she scurried out of her way, Michelle noticed unshed tears shining in the woman's blue eyes. Remorse niggling at her conscience, she strengthened her resolve by thinking about the blonde's designs on Cale. *She is pretty open about spending the night with George. Maybe she's hedging her bets and figures he's her fall back if Cale really isn't interested. More the fool her; my brother the gigolo has more women than you can shake a stick at. She's barking up the wrong tree on this one.*

The men brought a rush of cold air in from the mud room with them. Laughing at some shared joke, they plunked themselves at the table. Surreptitiously, she watched her brother smile and Stacey's face suddenly glow like a million watt bulb. She laid her hand on George's and twined her fingers with his. To Michelle's surprise, her brother grinned and scraped his chair closer to the woman. *Now, that's a first. This is usually where he puts his running shoes on.* She shook her head in bemusement. She never knew what her idiot brother would do next.

"When does your next hitch start?" Michelle broke the silence.

"We're shut down, maybe 'til after break-up." Her evil brother actually grinned at her, devilment in his brown eyes.

"Seriously? You're actually gonna be here to help with calving?" Another first.

"I was thinking of heading for Arizona or Cally and see what the circuit is like down there." He managed to look sheepish and belligerent as the same time.

"I don't think so, Tim!" She used a favourite phrase of Grampa's. "You can stick around here and help out for once."

"C'mon, Michelle, you've done it every other year, and I kinda promised Stacey I'd take her to Indio to watch some show jumping." He wheedled.

"Every other year I had Rob to help. It's only me now, or did that slip your mind? You want to go off gallivanting to Palm Desert and leave me here pulling calves in the snow by myself?" Michelle blinked her eyes to fend off tears. It was maddening that she cried when she was really angry. "Since when do you like show jumping?"

She saw her brother flick a glance at Cale and raise his eyebrows, maybe expecting his fellow male to throw him a life line.

"Leave me out of this." Cale held his hands up in surrender. "I'm not sticking my nose in the middle of this one."

"We could stay, George. I don't really need to go to Indio. Sara will post video on her website, so I can see how her horse is going." Stacey broke into the conversation.

"That's sweet, Stace, but I promised I take you." George kissed her knuckles.

"You promised her? Since when does a promise you made to a one night stand mean a tinker's damn?" Michelle spluttered. *What is wrong with the man? He's acting like he's going to live up to his words for once.*

"Michelle," George thundered, using his I'm-the-big-brother voice.

"Don't *Michelle* me. You think I've been blind to the string of broken hearts you've left all over Alberta and who knows where else. You love 'em and then move on; you always do." She fired back.

145

Stacey leaped to her feet, wrenching her hand free of George's grip and ran out of the room. The hammer of her racing feet sounded above them before a door slammed.

"For God's sake, Michelle, what is wrong with you?" George glared at her and headed for the hallway.

He only made it to the door before Stacey came charging down the hall and smacked into him. Hindered by the duffle bag she clutched in her hands, she pushed ineffectually at his body blocking the way. Her hair fell over her face, and she refused to look at George.

"Move," she demanded, her voice thick with tears.

"You need to listen to me...stop it." He took her shoulders and shook her slightly.

"Let go of me and move." Hysteria edged her voice, and Michelle could hear the sobs between the words.

"No, not until you listen to me. Michelle's just jealous because she thinks you have ideas about Cale. You need to let me explain." George let go of one shoulder to raise her chin with his free hand.

"You bastard." Michelle looked for something to hurl at his head. *How dare he say that, especially in front of Cale.*

"Shut up, Michelle. You've done enough damage for one day." Her brother didn't look at her. He turned Stacey with gentle hands and led her into the living room, closing the door behind him.

146

Michelle let fly with the empty mug she held in her hand. The sound of shattering pottery brought Storm crawling from under the table crying. Michelle dropped to her knees and gathered the shaking dog into her lap. Tears of embarrassment welled in her eyes.

"Real mature, Michelle." George's voice carried from the living room.

"Oh, piss off." She muttered and buried her face in the dog's fur.

# Chapter Ten

The scuffle of Cale's stocking feet on the linoleum reminded her he was still sitting at the table. The chair scraped as he stood. Michelle couldn't look at him, keeping her face in Storm's long fur. He must think she was a real witch to act like this, even worse Gramma would be furious with her behaviour.

"Maybe I should just go, or do you want me to stay?" Cale's voice was uncertain.

"Think you sticking around might prevent a murder?" Her voice was muffled by the dog in her arms.

"Don't know. I thought leaving might help me avoid a mug to the head."

*Evil man.* He was laughing at her. She raised her head and glared at him; the wary expression on his face brought a reluctant smile to her lips. His body appeared tense and ready to run for the hills if she picked up a piece of ammunition.

"If you're smiling, does that mean you're not planning on using me for target practice?" His smile warmed his eyes, and a dimple appeared at the corner of his mouth.

"You're safe for now, I guess." Michelle released Storm and got to her feet.

"Do you want to hang around here, or run into the steakhouse in Longview for something to eat?" His gaze strayed to the closed door of the living room.

"Longview sounds good to me, anywhere but here right now." Michelle grabbed her coat from the back of the chair.

"She really is just an old friend. Stacey isn't important to me in any other way." His eyes met hers earnestly. He stopped on the step below her, so Michelle didn't have to look up at him.

"Didn't look that way the other night." Her voice sounded obstinate even to her.

"I told you before. You can either believe me or not. I'm not going to tell you again." She heard him sigh before he turned and walked to his truck.

Michelle let Storm into the cab and climbed in after her. In silence, they drove out the lane and down the snow covered road to town. The steak house was full, so they settled for the hotel further north on Morrison Road. Storm thumped in beside them and arranged herself under a table in the corner. Michelle stared at her in surprise. The dog seemed quite at home, as if she visited the hotel bar often. Shrugging, she ordered her meal and wandered over to the table the dog had chosen. Cale followed her when their food was ready and set hers on the table. Michelle lifted her hand in recognition to a waitress. The woman was the mother of one of the girls she went to school with.

Stella stopped on her way by their table and stared at Storm. She peered under the table at the dog and held out her hand.

"Cassie, is that you?" The waitress spoke to the black dog, who wriggled out from between Michelle's legs and shoved her nose into the woman's hand.

"How do you know the dog?" Michelle laid her hand on Storm's head.

"She used to come in with Henry all the time. This was their table." Stella shook her head.

"Who's Henry? Henry Laskin? I didn't know he had a dog."

"Henry Ackerman from over Turner Valley way. He liked to come here 'cause this is where he met his wife." The woman's eyes looked shiny. "How did you come by Cassie?"

"I found her under my porch just before Christmas. Looked like someone beat on her, she was a mess." Michelle frowned.

"That son of Henry's, arrogant son of a bitch," she swore.

"What's the son got to do with it?" Cale broke in.

"Henry passed on the middle of December, and I offered to take the dog. I got to know Henry pretty good over the years, and a neighbor let me know when he died. The son said he'd take care of Cassie, and I never heard any more about it." She stroked the dog's head.

"He took care of her all right. Dumped her on the highway with a load of pups in her belly." Michelle ground her teeth in anger.

"Bastard, seemed like the type. Made a big deal about her being a papered purebred, near as I can tell she don't look like no purebred to me."

"My guess is she's purebred mutt." Cale interjected.

"You're gonna keep her are you?" Stella eyed Michelle sternly.

"Yup, we've been through a lot together. And if mister high and mighty son wants her back, there's about five thousand dollars in vet bills he'll have to take care of before he gets his hands on her." Michelle fisted her hand on the table.

Stella patted her hand. "He ain't gonna hear about her from me."

"Thanks, Stella."

"No problem, sweetie. I'm just glad Cassie is okay. What did you call her?"

"Storm."

"Storm it is then. Cassie must have run off and died somewhere in this weather. If that skunk comes looking for her, that's what I'll tell him." Stella moved on to wait on a new customer.

"You ready to go home?" Cale set his empty coffee mug on the scarred table.

Stubbornness tied a knot in her gut. She couldn't go back to the house and live with George and Stacey making cow's eyes at each other. There was no place else though. Mary would tell her to grow up and face the music if she went there. Michelle wasn't in the mood to face any music. Besides, who was George to think he could show up and run the show? He was quite content to leave her to it when he was working and not worry about how she managed.

"I'm not going back there."

"Okay…where do you want to go?"

"I don't know," she mumbled.

"What about Doc's? We have to pick up the puppies anyway."

"Mary won't get in the middle of a fight between me and George. She'll tell me to go home and work it out. I guess we do need to stop and get the puppies though." Michelle reluctantly got up from the table.

"Maybe you'll think of something on the way."

Michelle waved to Stella and followed Cale out of the hotel, Storm thumping along beside her. The short drive to Mary's was quiet; what was there to say? There was no way in hell she would stay at the ranch with lovebirds. Her stomach rolled at the thought. *It's so unfair… I bust my butt, and he just walks in and dictates what happens like he's king shit. Where does he get off?*

"You planning to murder someone?" Cale's voice startled her.

"What?" She blinked at him.

"You planning on murdering someone? If looks could kill, whoever it is would be dead right now. It's not me, is it?" The look on his face brought a smile to her lips.

"You're safe, Vet Boy. It's my brother who needs to look out."

152

Cale brought the truck to halt in Doc's drive, effectively ending the conversation. A fact, she was extremely grateful for. She sounded like a spoiled brat, but it didn't change how she felt to acknowledge it. Storm hopped down the walk ahead of her, no doubt anxious to reunite with her brood. The dog was sprawled in the middle of the floor with puppies squirming over her by the time Michelle entered the kitchen. Mary got up and poured coffee for the new arrivals.

"Can't stay long, Michelle. I'm on call tonight, and I've gotta get home and switch trucks." Cale drank his coffee standing by the counter.

"You and George have another fight?" Mary asked point blank.

"Why would you think that?" Michelle countered, knowing whose side Mary would be on.

"He called here three times this afternoon looking for you...that usually means you two are feuding, and you've hightailed it without finishing it." Mary smiled and patted her hand.

"He's a jackass," she said succinctly.

"You'll figure it out when you get home." Mary's tone indicated the matter was settled.

"I'm not going back there." Michelle radiated rebellion.

"Where are you gonna go, sweetness?" Doc said gently.

"Anywhere but there. I'll go the Bluebird before I go home," she said stubbornly.

153

"I don't think they allow dogs in the motel." Mary frowned at her.

"I'll find somewhere. There are lots of places in Okotoks or Blackie."

"Chelly, quit actin' like a child and go straighten this out with your brother." The older woman's voice left no room for argument.

"We got to get moving anyway. I'll get Cale to drop me off."

She pushed back from the table, gathered the puppies into the kennel, and with Storm in tow, left the house.

"What has gotten into that girl?" Mary's voice followed her down the walk.

Michelle stowed the puppies in the back seat and helped Storm unto the blanket beside the kennel. She slammed the door with more force than was necessary and stared out the windshield. When Cale entered the cab, she couldn't look at him. He must think she was an idiot. Why couldn't anyone understand how she felt? Tears formed in her eyes, and her throat hurt. *I will not cry in front of him. I won't.* In spite of her good intentions, frustration forced tears to overflow and course down her face. She brushed them away, anger rising in her chest. *Where am I going to go? I'm not staying with George and the blonde bimbo.* From the corner of her eye, she saw the dark-haired vet look over at her uncertainly. She held her breath and waited for the lecture Mary was sure to have told him to impart. To her relief, the man had the good sense to keep his own counsel and return his attention to the road.

The truck slowed as they approached the ranch gate, Cale put in the clutch and rolled slowly toward the entrance.

"What are we doing? Are you going in, or will you bolt the minute I leave?"

Startled he read her intentions so accurately, she said the first thing on her mind. "I can't. There's no way I'm watching them hang all over each other."

"Why do you feel so strongly about it? I would have thought you'd be glad your brother was happy?"

"I'm not sure. It's just he's gone most of the time, and every time he comes home, it's like everything I've done while he's gone is wrong. He walks in and takes over; everything has to be done his way. I'm tired of him ordering me around and then disappearing for twenty-eight days at a time and leaving me to cope with the weather and the harvest and the repairs..." She leaned her head against the window.

"Okay then, not the ranch." He was silent for a moment, "You can bunk in one of the spare rooms at my place if you want, unless there are too many memories there."

"Really, you wouldn't mind? It'll feel kind of weird, but I'd sure appreciate it."

He let the clutch out and continued down the road, leaving the ranch road behind. Michelle tried to control her wayward thoughts as they drove the familiar road winding along the headland and around the curve of the big coulee. It was so strange to see the old sign missing from the gate as they turned into the Chetwynd ranch. She corrected herself—Cale's ranch.

"Are you planning on changing the name of the place?"

"Eventually, just haven't got around to it yet. It'll be the Chetwynd place until I've lived here fifty years anyway." He laughed.

"Yeah, I suppose that's true isn't it?" She grinned back.

He parked the truck in the yard and looked at her with a strange expression on his face.

"Honey, we're home." His joking words sounded oddly prophetic.

## Chapter Eleven

The wind rattled the panes in the old window. The resulting drafts of cold air swirled around her when she opened the door. Michelle dropped her coat on the bed and surveyed the small room. A few steps brought her to the only window, and she spared a glance at the corrals below. Empty of life, the scene was lonely and sad with the wind whirling snow devils over the frozen earth. With a swift movement, she pulled the curtain to cut the force of the wind which found its way through the cracks. Her fingers stroked the material. Mrs. Chetwynd's mother made the curtains more years ago than Michelle could remember. Why the hell couldn't things just stay the same? Gramma Harner would be dead three years this June. Michelle could hear the woman's voice as clear as if she stood in the room with her. *Mark my words, Chelly, make sure Rob is what you really want. Don't go hitching your horse to his wagon just 'cause you've worshipped the boy since you could talk.* A small smile tugged at the corner of her mouth. Gramma Harner and her own gramma both warned her about Rob's wild ways. Naively, she thought he would change once they were married, and he had the ranch to look after.

"You were righter than you knew, ladies." Michelle's words painted strings of frost in the cold air.

Briskly, she rubbed her arms to warm them, and picking her coat up off the quilt covered bed, she shrugged it on. Old farm houses and central heat never seemed to be able to decide to be friends. The ancient furnace in the basement coughed and rumbled to life, but the air from the heat vent was only slightly warmer than the air in the room. Leaving the uninviting cold, Michelle poked her head into what used to be Cara's room. Rob's sister painted the room bright pink and purple the year she turned thirteen and somehow never got around to redecorating. Michelle shut the door and moved to the next one.

The room was on the south side of the building and noticeably warmer than the first. The bed was made up, and her breath was no longer visible. It used to belong to the hired hand, so the furnishings weren't fancy, just the bed, a dresser and the wash stand. It suited her just fine. The view to the south looked up the coulee with the snow covered prairie beyond where the valley turned west with the river.

"There you are. I thought I'd lost you." Cale stood in the doorway with an electric heater in his hand. "You're gonna need this. The old furnace is on its last legs, and the heat doesn't really get up to the second floor."

"So I noticed. Is it okay with you if I use this room?"

"Sure, if you want. There's the den downstairs where it's warmer if you're interested."

"I think I'll try this one for now. I like the view, and it's away from the wind."

"Suit yourself. I turned the old parlour into my bedroom until I can get the heat fixed. It's right over the furnace, so the hot air doesn't have far to go." He set the heater on the floor and grinned before disappearing into the hall.

She heard his boots on the stairs and left the window to collect the heater and plug it into the wall socket. It hummed to life, the centre glowing cherry red like a big sun. Holding her cold hands in the warmth, she took stock of the room. The dresser would do for the few clothes she had. Tomorrow would be time enough to go back home and collect her things. She opened the bottom drawer of the dresser and pulled out a thick quilt. Pausing for a moment, she thought about her Gramma who always kept the spare blankets in the bottom drawer of the dresser in the spare rooms. Apparently Mrs. Chetwynd belonged to the same school of thought.

Michelle folded the blanket and fashioned a bed for Storm and her puppies near the warmth of the heater. She pulled the curtain on the darkening sky to shut out the gathering cold.

Clattering down the stairs, she made a bee line for the kitchen where the wood stove was sending out delicious waves of warmth. Cale turned from the cupboard with a box of macaroni dinner in his hand and a sheepish look on his face. A pot of water boiled on the stove, and Michelle hurried to turn the burner to a lower heat before it bubbled over onto the stove top.

"This is the best I can offer you. I haven't had time to get groceries lately." Cale handed her the box with an apologetic grin.

"Beggars can't be choosers. It looks good to me."

"Better than eating crow and apologizing to Stacey?" The vet quirked his eyebrow at her and took a step back.

"Hell will freeze over first." She glowered and dumped the pasta into the rolling water.

"It's not Stacey's fault, Michelle, and for what it's worth I think your brother really cares about her."

"You don't know my brother like I do. He's all roses and wine until the thrill of the chase wears off and it gets boring. He runs like a deer the second one of them gets even a tiny bit serious. I've seen it way too many times to think this is anything different."

"It's still not Stacey's fault, and I think you owe her an apology."

"Why, because she's a friend of yours?"

The silence in the kitchen spoke louder than any words he could have said. Michelle turned with the wooden spoon in her hand and met the dark-haired man's gaze. Her first instinct was to tell him to go to hell, and she opened her mouth to do just that. Her anger died as quickly as it flared, and she turned back to the stove.

"Okay, maybe I was rough on her. It just infuriates me George's women can't see through the bullshit and leave him nursing a broken heart once in a while."

"So, you'll say you're sorry for screaming at her like a fish wife?" Cale pressed her.

"Fine, yes, I'll go make nice tomorrow when I get my things and bring the stock over." She relented.

"Stock? You want to bring the cattle over here?"

"No, just my two horses and the chickens. George can take care of the cattle and the rest of the horses; according to him, they're his anyway."

Michelle dumped the cheese mix into the strained macaroni, added butter and some milk before stirring the mixture and bringing the pot to the table.

"The barn is empty, and I think some of the corrals are still in working order. Come spring, I've got a lot of work to do around here."

Cale brought two cans of cola to the table and sank into a chair with a heavy sigh. "If I'd known just how rundown this place was, I would have dickered more on the price."

"Yeah, Rob kind of let the place go to hell in a hand basket after his folks moved to town. He was off following the circuit, and there were way more glamorous things to do than fix fences and bang on shingles." Michelle got the ketchup from the fridge and set it by the plates before sitting in the chair next to Cale.

"So how long are you planning to hide out here?" The words were slurred by his mouthful of macaroni.

"As long as you'll let me, and didn't your momma ever tell you not to talk with your mouth full?" She giggled.

"You can stay until you patch things up with your brother. Mary's gonna be mad at me for not making you work things out and offering you a refuge instead. She told me it's time you quit running and dealt with your problems. Her words not mine." He held up his hands in a mock attempt to protect himself.

"Mary should mind her own business," she replied with a snort. "She always favours George 'cause he can wrap her around his little finger."

"So long as you make things right with Stacey tomorrow, I have no objections to you staying here. The neighbours might talk though, you know."

"They can think what they want as far I'm concerned. This is the twenty-first century, not 1963 for heaven's sake."

They finished the meal in silence. Michelle scraped the leftovers into Storm's dish and ran her hand over the dog's head. The shrill of the phone broke the comfortable stillness, and instinctively she reached out to answer it.

"Chetwynd Ranch." The words rolled off her tongue before she stopped to think. Dead silence answered her.

162

"I'm looking for Cale Benjamin. This is the number he gave me." The voice sounded confused.

"No, this is the right place. Hang on a sec, and I'll get him for you."

She handed the phone to Cale with an apologetic grimace. He took the receiver and pushed himself back from the table before he answered.

"Dr. Benjamin here. Oh hey, Mom, no this is the right number. Michelle just made a mistake when she answered the phone."

He was silent for a few minutes, listening to whatever his mother was saying and rolling his eyes.

"She's my closest neighbour, Mom; don't go reading more into than there is."

Michelle rose from the table and gathered the dishes to carry to the sink. The heat rose in her face, and she knew it was bright red. Now his mother would think they were involved. The last thing she needed was another matchmaker like Mary. Her hands stilled in the water at the sudden thought, maybe his mother didn't like the idea of some woman being alone with her son. What if she thought Stacey was the perfect person for Cale? She resumed washing but couldn't stop the train of her thoughts. What did it matter anyway? She wasn't interested in Cale that way. She wasn't, she told herself sternly. Men were trouble, pure and simple. She jumped as Cale put his hand on her shoulder and ducked her head to hide the blush she knew stained her cheeks.

"Sorry, about that. My mom's radar was going off, happens anytime there's a woman in proximity to me she thinks it might be 'the one'." His soft laughter warmed her heart in a way she couldn't explain.

"Good thing she doesn't know I'm bunking here." She smiled over her shoulder and set the last plate on the dish rack.

"Umm, yeah…her and Dad are coming on New Year's Eve to see the place and take stock of what needs fixing. They're gonna notice you're staying here."

"I can clear out if you want," she offered.

"I don't mind if you don't. It's kind of nice to think there's someone here when I get home. Keep the home fires burning and all that."

"What if they hate me?"

"Why in heaven's name would they hate you, silly woman?" He ran his hand over her hair.

"Maybe your mom thinks Stacey is better for you than someone she doesn't know?"

Cale's laughter made her spin around and glare at him. "Mom told me in no uncertain terms if I married Stacey some village just lost their idiot. I never had any intention of marrying the girl. We were never more than friends."

"I don't want to be in the way when your folks are here though."

"If I thought you would be in the way, I'd tell you. I'd like it if you stayed and met my parents. Mom is gonna love Storm, and we might get a home for a couple of puppies."

Michelle raised her eyes to meet his warm brown gaze and nodded her head, not trusting her voice at the moment. Cale placed his hands on her shoulders and pulled her against his broad chest. After a second's hesitation, she wrapped her arms around his waist and rested her head on his shoulder. She felt him sigh, and the whisper of his breath on her hair a moment before his lips touched her temple. They were warm and soft against her skin. Michelle let her eyes drift closed and smiled into his shirt. His mouth traveled across her cheekbone. She tilted her head and sought his lips with her own.

The touch of his mouth on hers sent molten fire through her limbs, and somehow she forgot to breath. The world narrowed to the heat of his body against hers and the hardness of his muscles under her fingers. In response to his deepening kiss, she allowed a hand to drop from his waist and caress the hard muscles of his butt. She smiled against his lips when his body leaped at her touch and purred in her throat as his hand trailed down her collarbone and cupped her breast in his palm.

She loved the way his body reacted to her, shoving her hands into the back pockets of his jeans, she stroked his ass and was rewarded by the press of his hips against hers. Cale brushed the sensitive peak of her bosom with his thumb, and Michelle fought to control the rush of heat pooling in her groin. She resisted for a moment before giving in and letting the delicious fire run through her veins. Freeing her hands, she grasped his shirt above the belt of his jeans and pulled it free. She giggled when he jumped as her cold hands met his hot body.

"Christ, Michelle. Are you trying to kill a man, putting cold hands on him like that?"

"You know what they say, Vet Man, cold hands, warm heart."

She ran her hands up the cords of muscle on his broad back. A small squeal escaped her lips when his broad hand cupped her buttock, his fingers slipping in to touch the heat between her thighs. Her fingers closed convulsively on his shoulders while his hands woke a fierce passion that threatened to drown her with its intensity. The world narrowed and consisted of nothing except the touch of his fingers on her body and the response she aroused from his heated flesh.

An annoying vibration on her hipbone registered a split second before Cale removed his lips from her neck. Cursing softly under his breath, he dug in the front pocket of his jeans for something. Michelle floated in a peaceful bliss, her fingers toying with the hard button of his nipple while her head rested on his shoulder. His hand captured her errant fingers and gave her a tiny shake. She shook her head and moved away from him slightly to process the chain of events she was engaged in. *What am I doing behaving like this? I'm not some buckle bunny looking to put notches on my belt, for God's sake. I've never acted this way before, even with Rob. What is wrong with me?*

Extricating herself from his arms, she turned back to the sink and the dishes. Vaguely she was aware of sound of his voice speaking to someone on the cellphone.

"I'll be there in twenty minutes. Meet me at the clinic." His voice was calm and businesslike.

"What's up?" She turned to face him with the dishcloth in her hand.

"McIntyre's have a heifer in trouble. She's way early, and it sounds like the calf is hip locked." Cale drew on his boots and coat while he spoke. Pointing his key fob out the window, he was rewarded by the mighty Dodge springing to life.

"Can you call Doc and let him know to expect McIntyre, and that I'm on my way?"

He stopped in the doorway and fixed her with a long look which stirred up the emotions from a few moments earlier all over again.

"We'll finish our conversation later, Michelle."

"There wasn't much talking going on." She snorted.

"I gotta go; we will talk later."

His promise hung in the air after he left. She watched the taillights of the truck disappear down the lane and reappear on the other side of the coulee where the road looped back before passing her place. *George's place*, she reminded herself. The warm lights winked through the blowing snow. How many times had she imagined this scene?

In her daydreams, she was the mistress of the house, filling it with children and the aroma of baking bread and cookies. Sitting down to dinner after a hard day of work, with the four kids she always wanted, and her handsome husband waiting to cut the roast. She would look out the big window to the house across the coulee where she grew up and feel connected to both her old life and her new one. Her daydream eyes looked down the table, past her three sons and one daughter to smile at her handsome Cale.

"Cale?" The sound of her startled exclamation broke the spell of her favourite daydream.

Unsettled and disturbed, she turned back to the washing up. Rob, it was Rob who was supposed to smile back at her from the head of the table, his eyes promising pleasant things in the dark quiet of their room later. Rob, not Cale.

Closing her eyes, Michelle concentrated on Rob, attempting to bring his familiar features into focus. Her inner eye refused to cooperate, and Cale's face looked back her, refusing to be displaced. What was it about the man? How could he make her feel like this when she had only known him such a short while? He made her feel things she never knew existed. Kissing Rob and loving Rob paled in comparison to the emotions which rocked her just by being near Cale.

*I wonder if Gramma was right, and Rob was just a habit I never out grew? I guess I should have listened to her more. I never felt anything like this when I was with Rob, even when we had makeup sex after he'd go chasing some buckle bunny. Why did I put up with it? Gramma and Mary both told me, I just didn't hear.*

"Mary...crap, I forgot to call Doc."

Her hand was trembling as she dialled the familiar number. The realization she so misunderstood her relationship with Rob irritated her. The fact Cale could reduce her to mush scared the heck out of her.

"Doc, hey it's Michelle. Cale is on his way in to the clinic to meet McIntyres. They're bringing in a heifer he thinks is gonna need a C-section." She delivered the information quickly, hoping Doc wouldn't ask why she was calling for Cale.

"Got it, Chelly. I'll go turn the lights on in the clinic and get things ready just in case. Everything okay? Why are you calling from Cale's and not home? You and George still feuding?"

"Something like that; I gotta go, Doc." Michelle hung up quickly and pressed her cold hands to her hot cheeks.

She finished the washing up and tidied the rest of the kitchen. The floors needed a good scrub, and the curtains would have to come down and get bleached to return them to the original white. Maybe she should just get new ones. She mentally kicked herself—this wasn't her house to buying curtains for.

Flicking off the overhead light, she left the small lamp by Cale's makeshift desk burning. The puppies were sleeping in their bed by the stove, and Storm looked up with her big brown eyes, pleading for a respite from the voracious youngsters. Michelle laughed softly and gestured with her hand to indicate to Storm she could follow her upstairs if she liked. The black dog got carefully to her feet and limped over to push her head into Michelle's hand.

At the bottom of the stairs, she gathered the dog in her arms and carried her up. Once in her room, she set the dog on the bed. Storm turned around once before curling up with a sigh on the side next the wall. Michelle shed her clothes quickly in the chilly air and climbed under the covers. Rolling over, she pulled the blankets from under Storm and flipped them over her. She snuggled the dog against her body to share the warmth. One minute she was thinking about Cale and the McIntyre's heifer, and the next she was asleep.

# Chapter Twelve

Cale was nowhere in sight when Michelle entered the kitchen in answer to the high pitched demand of the puppies for their mother. Storm padded in behind her and made a beeline for the yelping creatures. Blessed silence settled over the room, the screeching replaced by loud slurps and the occasional tiny growl from the squirming mass of black fur. Michelle smiled as Storm lay down on her side with a sigh. Filling her mug from the pot on the counter, she moved to the table and picked up the note which was anchored under the sugar jar.

Cale's writing was dark and spikey and amazingly legible for a doctor. He was out on another call already this cold morning. The keys for the farm truck were under the note, so she could pick up the chickens and her horses. She shivered as she surveyed the wintry grey farm yard. Finishing her coffee, she rose and shrugged into her outdoor clothes. It would be nice to have the rest of her belongings with her, she thought, pulling on the only pair of gloves she had.

Leaving Storm and the puppies in peace, she hurried outside and fired up the old red farm vehicle. Fortunately, Cale thought to plug it in for her, and it turned over without too much protest. She set the heater on full blast and scurried back to the relative warmth of the house. Michelle looked through the window toward the ranch on the far side of the coulee to see if George's truck was still there. With any luck at all, she could be there and gone before he knew it. The last thing she felt like this morning was another go round with her pig-headed brother.

Although, she supposed, she did promise to apologize to Stacey. She ran her hand over her face in exasperation. In all fairness, she probably did owe the girl one, but it rankled just the same. Of all the women George could have picked up and brought home, why did it have to be her? She could see Mary's hand in this from the get go. *Well, the woman will have a hay day with the news I'm staying at Cale's*. The thought brought a wry smile to her face.

With one last glance out the window in the direction of her ranch, Michelle wasted no time in getting from the warm house to the dubious warmth of the truck cab. Surprisingly for an old beast, it threw a decent amount of heat. The keys for her truck were in her pocket, so she would leave the farm truck at George's for now and bring her own vehicle back with the trailer. Deftly sliding the manual transmission into first she drove out of the yard.

A short time later, she was turning into the familiar drive and bumping toward the main house. George's truck was missing, and she heaved a sigh of relief. Sliding the truck into the spot beside her own, Michelle parked and jumped out. She made short work of sliding the coupler into the socket for the trailer and hooking up. Rubbing her hands together to warm them, she headed for the tack room to collect her saddles, bridles and grooming equipment. A ruckus from the hen house drew her attention as she exited the barn. She hurried to dump the load of tack she carried into the dressing room of the trailer.

Slamming the door, Michelle went to investigate the problem in the chicken house. *If George left the door open, and the coyotes got in—*

Her thought was interrupted by a series of high pitched female screams. She reached the door of the hen house, jumping back as it flew open. Stacey emerged flapping her arms and screeching. Michelle took one look and doubled over with laughter. Stacey was bent over with three hens on her shoulders and another on the back of her head. She beat at them with her hands, which only made the hens scream back at her. The three on her shoulders gave up the fight and jumped down with a flurry of wings and a large amount of chicken complaining. The fourth hen, frantic to get away from the crazy human, flapped her wings and screamed with her feet caught in Stacey's long hair.

Michelle controlled her hysteria long enough to shoo the three hens back into the coop and fasten the door. She turned back to Stacey who was still screaming and trying to reach the hen on the back of her head.

Amusingly, the hen was upset enough to have deposited a white stream of chicken excrement down the woman's back. Michelle bit her lip to stop her giggles.

"Stand still and shut up, will you." She approached Stacey cautiously.

"Get it off; get it off. For the love of God, get it off me."

The woman stopped screaming and flailing her arms and stood bent over. A tiny bit of guilt blossomed in Michelle when she realized tears were falling from Stacey's eyes into the snow.

"Here now, chicken girl, stay put and let me get you loose."

Speaking easily and calmly, she captured the bird's wings and worked the horny feet free from the long blonde hair tangled around them. Finishing the task, she tucked the bird under her arm.

"There, you're free. What were you doing in there in the first place?"

Stacey straightened up, wiping the tears from her face and pushing her hair back. A grimace crossed her face when her fingers encountered the slimy white liquid on the back of her head.

"Gross. You stupid chicken." She looked like she was going to start crying all over again.

"Why were you in there?"

"I wanted to prove to George I could be helpful here and take care of things while he's working."

Her lower lip trembled, and a look of defeat crossed her face. To her credit, in Michelle's eyes, she stood straighter, and a look of defiance entered her eyes.

"You won't have to worry about the hens. I'm taking them with me. You can tell George that when he gets home."

"Where are you going? George said you'd be back this morning, and you two would work things out."

"George thought wrong. I'm out of here. The hens are mine and the two horses. He can straighten up with me for the cattle when they go to market."

While she spoke, Michelle took the hen back to the coop and set her with the others. Briskly, she pulled the cages from inside a storage shed and started transferring the hens from the building into the wire containers.

"Michelle, I don't want to be the cause of a feud between you and your brother. Won't you at least stay and talk to him?"

"There's nothing to talk about. This has been coming a long time. He comes home and starts bossing me around. It's his way or the highway, but where is he when it's minus forty in March, and the cows are calving. Not here, that's for sure."

She carried the hens to the trailer and placed the containers on the floor in the front. Sliding the divider into place, she went to get her horses. Stacey trailed along behind her with a bewildered look on her face.

"But where are you going? Can George get a hold of you at Doc's?"

The woman was persistent; Michelle would give her that. Ignoring the questions, she led both horses toward the open trailer, throwing the shanks over their withers as they got close. Both mares obligingly walked on, and she closed the gate behind them. Hoping Stacey would get the hint, she opened the truck door to step in.

"Michelle, don't leave like this. I'm sorry I made you angry." The blonde's voice broke.

With a sigh, Michelle turned and leaned against the truck. "I'm not mad at you; it's George. He goes through women like other men change their socks. He comes and goes as he pleases and leaves everyone else to pick up the pieces. I'm tired of cleaning up his messes."

"I thought you were mad at me 'cause Cale and I are friends. We really are just friends."

"Look, I'm sorry I acted like I did last night. It's not your fault. Be careful about your relationship with my brother. Don't get burned too badly."

Michelle swung up into the seat and turned the key in the ignition. Irritation coursed through her as she remembered she still had to collect her clothes from the house. Jumping back down, she slammed the door and headed for the house.

"I'm just gonna get my clothes. Anything else George can have, or I'll come get when I find a place of my own." She flung the words over her shoulder. Stacey trailed along behind her.

"Can I help you with anything?" The blonde stood in the centre of the kitchen with a lost look on her face. "What should I tell George when he gets back? Where can he reach you?"

"He's got my cell. He can call me on it if he needs to." She took the stairs two at a time while she spoke.

In short order, Michelle packed everything she needed for the time being and loaded it into her truck. She climbed in and rolled down the window to be polite as Stacey followed on her heels.

"Tell George I'll come and pick up Cale's farm truck later today or tomorrow. You really should go have a shower and get the chicken crap out of your hair." She allowed a small smile to cross her lips.

"Where are you going?"

"Cale's, over at the old Chetwynd place."

She rolled forward and let out the clutch as she spoke. Amusement spiked through her at the astounded expression on Stacey's face. *Put that in your pipe and smoke it, blondie.*

# Chapter Thirteen

The short drive back to Cale's place gave her some time to think about what needed to be done. There was straw and hay in the pole barn, and she would need to run into the UFA for some feed this afternoon. The neglected appearance of the frame house greeted her critical gaze as the rig rattled to a halt in the yard. Cale's parents were coming in two days, and the place looked like a pig sty. The peeling paint and the overgrown garden and flower beds would have to wait for spring. It was too cold to do anything about them now. The inside of the place wasn't much better, she reflected. Once the stock was settled, she would have to get started on the living room and the kitchen for sure. Not to mention making sure there were no resident mice in the largest of the spare rooms upstairs.

Briskly, Michelle set about sweeping out the chicken house which hadn't been touched since Mrs. Chetwynd moved to town. She hung the brooder lamps and set the timer on the white light to regulate the hours of artificial daylight needed to keep the hens laying through the short winter days. Scooping the frozen chicken turds out of the nesting boxes sent her into a paroxysm of sneezing, the fine dust rising in the cold air around her. It brought a smile to her lips at the memory of the hen in Stacey's hair. *Be nice, Michelle*, she chided mentally. The smile stayed on her face while she lugged the tub of refuse out of the henhouse and to the manure pile.

Leaving the tub by the pole barn, she threw three bales of straw unto a calf sled and skidded it across the icy ground to the chicken house. Before long, the yellow bedding brightened the small building, and it looked homey and inviting to her critical gaze.

"C'mon, chicken girls; your new home is ready."

The silly hens answered her with contented chuckling and clucks from their wire enclosures. It took another hour to get them settled with their food hopper full and the heated waterer filled and operational. A sense of happiness and satisfaction enveloped her. Sitting on the edge of the nesting box, her gaze tracked the tiny motes of dust floating in the air around her. *This is how I always imagined it would be when Rob and I took this place over. It was such a beautiful dream... Living here, raising our kids, watching them play where we played when we were that age... This always felt more like home than my own place did. No use crying over spilt milk.*

Banishing the melancholy thoughts, Michelle stood up and left the hens to explore their new home. Clipping the door securely behind her, she crossed the snowy yard and headed to the small barn to tackle the job of getting it ready for the mares. The sun came out from behind the clouds halfway across the open space. She changed direction and approached the trailer instead. Sliding the door open, she caught the lead lines off the horses' necks as they stepped from the box. She fished in her pocket and produced a horse cookie for each of them before leading them to a corral that was in relatively good repair. The mares came through the gate quietly and Michelle unclipped the lead rope from their halters. Leaving the halters on just in case the corral wasn't as sturdy as it looked, she looped the shanks around the gate posts and tied them securely. Returning to the trailer, she brought half a bale of hay and threw into the enclosure. The mares surveyed their surroundings and dropped their heads to the feed at their feet.

Satisfied the horses would be fine, Michelle approached the task waiting in the barn, feeling more settled than she had in a long time. She flicked on the light switch inside the door and was gratified to find it working. Grabbing a pitchfork and the old wheelbarrow standing in the first stall, she went about cleaning the stalls. It took the better part of the afternoon to finish the chore, and the sun was sinking below the western horizon by the time she emerged from the doorway.

The long rays slanted across the snowy prairie, turning the snow to liquid gold and orange. The remnants of the clouds flying low in the sky picked up subtle hues of salmon, saffron and magenta. A brisk wind whined in the hydro wires and drew her gaze to the north where a large purple and grey cloud bank dominated the view. The afterglow of the sunset provided enough light to make her way to the corral and collect the horses. They danced at her side as the wind picked up and whirled dust devils across the yard.

The interior of the barn was hushed and quiet after being in the rising wind outside. Michelle put the mares in stalls beside each other, the horses quickly finding the sweet feed in the mangers. Earlier, she put hay in both stalls and made sure the electric water bowls were functional, turning on the heat tape wrapping the pipes. She double latched the stall doors before venturing out into the wind to bring her tack from the trailer. She paused in the doorway to gauge the speed of the approaching storm front. The wall of clouds billowed and moved swiftly across the open prairie on the north side of the coulee.

Working quicker than she would have liked, Michelle moved her equipment into the tack room in record time. She positioned the last saddle rack and placed her trophy saddle carefully on it. The saddle was protected with a custom made cover embroidered with her name and the year she won high point barrel racer. The year she was on her way to the NFR, and she had to drop out when her dad got sick. *Water under the bridge.* The boom and rattle of the first fists of the storm hitting the barn sent her hurrying to the door. Fine, wind driven snow silvered in the frosty air. She pulled the door shut, secured it against the wind and then jogged to the trailer and closed all the doors before the wind could catch them and rip them off.

She slid into the cab of the truck and turned the ignition, there was a good place in the lee of the barn to park the rig where the snow didn't drift too badly. Quickly accomplishing her task she plowed through the wind and thickening snow to the house. Storm greeted her at the door, and Michelle let her out to do her business. She lingered by the door, knowing the black dog wouldn't be gone long. Sure enough, a minute later the snow-encrusted dog limped up the step. Shutting the door against the rising wind, she picked up an old towel from a trunk and brushed the worst of the snow off Storm.

Together they entered the warm kitchen, the puppies scrambling across the linoleum toward them. Their short legs were totally inadequate to hold their fat tummies off the ground. Storm shook herself and lay down on the thick hand-hooked rug by the wood stove, her offspring tumbling behind her on their stubby legs and big paws.

"They can start on some wet food next week, momma. Give you a break."

Michelle spoke to the patient mother while she put fresh wood in the belly of the stove and stirred the embers with a poker. Satisfied the wood would catch, she closed the stove and moved to the window. Heavy snow pelted the glass. It was too cold for the precipitation to be wet, but the dry fine flakes accumulated quickly on the ground. Already, drifts were forming across the lane where it curved to the east. She pulled the sleeves of her sweater over her cold hands and shivered. *It's a good night to be inside. I wonder when Cale will get home?*

A glance at the clock told her it was five o'clock. It was too early yet for the lengthening days to make much difference to the hours of daylight. Flicking on the radio she sang along:

*"Long and lean in tight blue jeans;*
*Is every cowgirl's dream*
*But don't trust him with your heart;*
*'Cause he'll only play the part..."*

She quit singing as she rummaged in the freezer for some stewing beef and added some potatoes, carrots, and onions which she unearthed from the depths of the cold room off the kitchen. The beef was sizzling in a pan, and the water just beginning to boil under the carrots and potatoes when the phone rang. Michelle jumped and pressed a hand to her heart. The howl of the wind and the sound of the snow hitting the house accentuated the fact she was alone. *It's not like you've never been alone in a storm before for heaven's sake*, she chided silently. Moving to the desk she plucked the phone from the cradle and answered it.

"Dr. Benjamin's." She hoped she sounded professional.

"Michelle dear, is that you? It's Peggy, Cale's mom."

"Umm, yes, hi it's me." She silently cursed the stutter in her voice.

"Is Cale around?"

"He's not home yet. I haven't heard from him all day. The weather looks like it's settling into blizzard again."

"Oh dear, we've had so much of it already, and it's not New Year's yet." Laughter tinkled from the phone.

"Is it snowing where you are yet? Do you want me to ask Cale to call you when he gets in?"

"No snow yet, but they're calling for it. Michelle, if you could just give him a message for me, I'd appreciate it."

"Sure, Mrs. Benjamin. Just let me get a pen."

"Oh my goodness, call me Peggy. Mrs. Benjamin is my mother-in-law."

"Okay…Peggy."

"Tell Cale that Carson and I will be arriving on the thirtieth. I hate travelling on New Year's Eve. I'm bringing a big turkey for dinner on the first. Did you want to invite your brother and Stacey to eat with us?"

The thirtieth…that only left two days to get the house in some sort of shape before Cale's parents arrived. Her frantic mind barely registered the last bit of the conversation.

"What time on the thirtieth? Oh, George and Stacey…I don't know…I'll have to ask them tomorrow. Do you want me to call and let you know?" Dinner with George and Stacey was not high on the list of things she wanted to do.

"Not until later in the day, dear. Probably late afternoon. You don't need to bother calling about Stacey and your brother. The bird is big enough if they can come, and if not, you and Cale can have leftovers for weeks." The woman's laugh was pleasant and warm and helped to soothe Michelle's tangled nerves.

"I'll let Cale know you called and when to expect you. I hope Doc is on call while you're here. I think they traded off Christmas for New Year's with each other."

"Well, if he's on call, it will give me some time to get to know you better, Michelle. Cale never tells me anything about his private life. That boy is as tight lipped as his father. You can fill me in on all the interesting details of your relationship. Bye for now, sweetie."

The woman disconnected before Michelle could get a word out. *What relationship? What did Cale tell his mother about me?*

Absently, she moved the pan of beef off the burner and turned the heat off under the vegetables. The steam wafted around her as she carried the pot to the sink and strained the water off. Adding some fresh water and setting the pot aside, Michelle retrieved the meat from the fry pan and added it to the carrots and potatoes. Deftly chopping a small onion she dropped it in as well. A quick look through the cupboards rewarded her with a box of cornstarch. In minutes, the stew was bubbling happily on the stove.

Michelle turned from sliding the batch of biscuits into the oven and caught the sweep of headlights cutting through the darkness of the yard. She frowned at the unexpected surge of happiness racing through her. *So Cale is home. Don't make more of this than it is. Have fun playing house, but remember this isn't for real. Just 'til you find a place of your own.*

The fact her hands were trembling when she reached for the dishes to set the table further annoyed her. *Get a grip.* The plates and cutlery were in place as a blast of cold air announced his arrival a moment before Cale stepped into the warm kitchen.

"Wow, something smells good. I could get used to this kind of treatment."

His smile stopped the breath in her throat. It wasn't fair the man could look so good with snow-plastered hair and blood on his coat. Unable to control her reaction, Michelle smiled back and moved across the floor to take his coat. She deposited it on top of the washing machine to wait for later. Cale removed his boots and set them by the wood stove. He knelt and stroked Storm's head. The dog regarded him with adoring eyes. With gentle hands, he unwound the dressing on her leg and examined it carefully.

"It doesn't look good, does it?" She hunkered down beside him.

186

"It should be healing quicker. The edges aren't pinking up at all. You might want to start thinking about alternatives." His warm brown gaze locked on her.

"Like…?."

"It might be kinder to amputate the limb and get her fitted with a prosthetic of some kind."

Michelle leaned closer and examined the gaping wound, the edges weren't coming together, and there was no granulation she could see. Bending nearer, she took a deep breath. The faint but unmistakable scent of necrosis met her nostrils.

"Can we do it while she's still nursing the puppies?"

Her fingers played with the soft hair on Storm's ears. She raised her gaze to Cale's when he put his hand over hers and squeezed gently.

"I'm not sure there's much of a choice. If we wait too long, and she gets septic, there won't be much of a chance of success given the state of her health."

"She's just starting to gain some flesh on her bones. Are you saying we should wean the puppies and do it in the next couple of days?"

"I think that's her best chance for a positive outcome. I guess the question is, are you willing to take on the chore of feeding the puppies. They only just got their eyes open, and it will be another seven days before you can get them off hand-feeding milk supplements and completely dependent on puppy food."

"I don't have a problem with taking care of them for her. I just want her to have the best chance of getting better. She's been through so much."

"It's too late to do anything tonight, and the roads are getting bad. I had to plow through a few drifts to get home."

The vet rebound the dog's leg while he spoke and sat back on his heels when he was done. Michelle stroked the fat round belly of one of the male puppies, tracing the white flash that ran from his throat to mid-belly. She shivered when Cale caught her hand in his warm fingers and brought them to his lips. Involuntarily, she moved closer to him; her thoughts focussed on the curve of his lips. Those lips moved closer, and his features became blurred. Michelle closed her eyes and inhaled the spicy scent of his aftershave mixed with an underlying aroma of horse and disinfectant.

Her mouth opened under his; the touch of his tongue tracing her bottom lip turned her bones to mush. She allowed herself to melt into his embrace, bringing her hand to his face, the stubble of his beard rough on her palm. The embrace deepened, and she ran her hands through his dark thick hair. His breath brushed her sensitive earlobe as he sighed and broke the kiss. She rested her forehead on his shoulder and took a second to catch her breath. Cale leaned against the wall. She turned and allowed him to pull her into the vee of his thighs. Her head fell back and she closed her eyes, the even rhythm of his breathing creating a warm fuzzy sense of security.

"Mmm, this is nice. Where have you been all my life?"

She snuggled closer, letting the warmth of his body seep into her. A smile touched her lips at the twitch his body made against her lower back. His warm breath caressed her cheek a second before he nuzzled the side of her neck, sending delicious shivers through her. His large hands came up and cradled her tingling breasts, stroking the flannel of her shirt.

"Waiting to meet you, you crazy woman."

She explored the taut muscles of his thighs with her fingers, while she floated on a sea of blissful sensation. In response to his searching fingers slipping inside her shirt and igniting fires of desire on her naked flesh, she turned her face up and met his lips. Nothing existed outside of his lips on hers and the feel of his hands on her flesh. Suddenly she remembered the phone call.

"I almost forgot, your mom called. They're coming on the thirtieth, late in the afternoon."

"What made you think of that right now?" The chuckle rumbled in her ear as it rose from his chest.

"She called just before you got in. We should eat. Dinner is probably cold by now."

Reluctantly, she scrambled to her feet and offered Cale a hand up. She heated the stew in the microwave and dished it out onto the plates. With a squeak of alarm, Michelle rescued the biscuits from the oven before they became useful only as hockey pucks.

"You think we should take her leg tomorrow, then?" Michelle brought the conversation back to Storm, regarding Cale across the table.

"Yeah, I think it's her best shot. It puts a lot of pressure on you though." His eyes crinkled at the corners with a small smile.

"It's not like I've got better things to do at the moment."

"I see the light is on in the shed. Did you get the hens settled okay?"

"All set. I put Bella and Jaz in the barn. I hope that's okay. The storm was blowing in, and I hate to leave them out in it if I have a choice."

"Use whatever out buildings you feel like, Michelle. Treat this place like your own as long as you're here."

There was a hint of something important hidden in his words; the heat rose in her face in answer to the unspoken invitation. Dropping her eyes to the stew, she avoided his searching gaze and applied herself to eating. The scrape of his chair as he rose to deposit the dishes in the sink broke her reverie.

"I'll just call Doc and let him know we'll bring Storm into the clinic in the morning. You and Mary can have a visit while we're in surgery."

The sound of his low voice calmed and reassured her ruffled nerves while she washed up the supper dishes. He hung up from Doc, and she heard him talking to his mother. Other than the first bit of conversation, she could only hear the soft drone of his voice. She looked at Storm sleeping peacefully with her babies, and her heart tightened in her chest. *Please let it be the right thing to do. Don't let it make her worse and put her through the pain for nothing.* Conflicting emotions warred within her. A strong desire to protect the dog from any more trauma fought with the knowledge the leg wasn't healing and would kill her if nothing was done. *The big question is, do I trust Cale? In my heart I know he's right. I have to get over this mistrust of men I seem to have developed. Not all men are George or Rob.*

"I picked up a movie on the way home; wanna watch it together?"

Cale took the dishcloth from her hand and plopped it on the counter. With a mischievous grin, he headed down the hall in the direction of the front room. Michelle shrugged and followed him, pausing in the doorway while she took in the scene which met her eyes. He had commandeered the room into a bedroom cum office. The old, worn couch was pushed against the wall, and a queen size bed sat on the far side of the room away from the big windows. The wall opposite the bed was occupied by a forty-

191

two-inch plasma TV; papers and paraphernalia spilled from the oak desk onto the floor. Cale leaned against the headboard, propped up on pillows with a big bowl of jelly beans and gummy worms beside him. He patted the bed and waggled his eyebrows at her.

"C'mon, there's plenty of room, and this is the warmest room in the house. I promise to be good."

She giggled and clambered onto the bed, wriggling until she had a comfortable nest hollowed out in the pillows. He reached out and put his arm around her shoulder, inviting her to lean on his broad chest. A small sound of contentment escaped her as she revelled in the warmth of his embrace. Storm stuck her head in the door and disappeared. She was back momentarily with a puppy in her jaws. After transferring all six puppies onto the dog bed in front of the television, she flopped down and promptly closed her eyes.

Cale fiddled with the remote and started the movie. To her surprise it wasn't a blood and guts guy flick, instead it was episodes of the English show about the life of a young vet starting out in a practice in Yorkshire. Michelle was having trouble keeping track of what was happening on the screen. Her eyes kept closing, and she kept missing the middle part of each episode.

## Chapter Fourteen

The sky was still dark when she opened her eyes, and for a moment, the surroundings puzzled her until she became aware of the rise and fall of Cale's chest under her head. She must have fallen asleep before the movie was over. He stroked her hair and shifted slightly to draw her closer. Michelle rubbed her cheek sensuously against the soft material of his shirt and slid her arm across his firm belly.

"Go back to sleep. We don't have to be to Doc's 'til nine-thirty. It's only half gone six right now." The timbre of his voice was deep and drowsy.

"You don't have calls this morning?"

"Nope. I'm off 'til day after New Year's." The man sounded smug and well-satisfied.

"How did you pull that off? Mary insists Doc is home for holiday dinners, barring a major catastrophe." She pushed herself upright and peered at him through sleep muzzy eyes.

"He hired a locum to take care of it. She graduates in May, and Doc is thinking of hiring her for the small animal clinic."

Cale kissed the tip of her nose and stretched his long frame before untangling himself from her arms and the blankets. Michelle snuggled deeper into the warmth of the bed, admiring the play of muscles in his back as he stripped off his shirt and dropped his jeans to the floor. Snagging his robe from the pile of clothes by the desk, he turned, and his gaze lingered on her face before he smiled. The emotion on his face sent waves of heat through her body, and her mouth trembled at little as she smiled in return.

"You look good in my bed."

The remark rang in her ears after he left the room. The sound of water running informed her he was taking a shower. Her mind presented her with images of soapy lather sluicing down the flat plane of his chest and lower over the enviable six pack. Her fingers twitched at the unbidden thought of running her hands over his slick physique, taking the weight of him in her palm. Her cheeks heated at the train of thought. She threw back the quilt and hurried up to her room before she gave in to the urge to join him in the shower.

"My stars, what has gotten into me?" Michelle spoke out loud, hoping it would get her mind out of the gutter. "The guy is too smokin' hot for my own good."

In record time, she dressed and returned to the main floor. She entered the kitchen and started the coffee before removing Storm's water and food bowl. The dog spent the night in Cale's room, so she hadn't put anything in her stomach since before midnight. Kneeling by the kennel, she straightened the padding inside so everything would be ready for the puppies when it was time to leave.

"You want some scrambled eggs and toast?"

Cale clattered the pots and pans as he searched for the skillet. Finding the one he was looking for, he set it on the burner. Efficiently, the large man retrieved eggs from the fridge and broke them into a pudding bowl before whisking them into a froth. Michelle finished with the kennel and moved to get the bread and toaster. Cale deftly got plates and utensils while keeping a watchful eye on the eggs.

"A man after my own heart, good looking, and he cooks, too." Michelle teased him while buttering the toast.

"Just so you know what I'm up to, woman." His face was more than half serious. "I meant it when I said you look good in my bed. You look good in my life."

"Where did that come from? I haven't even known you that long." The knife fell from her suddenly nerveless fingers.

"I've known Doc most of my life; my grandpa kept in touch for years. There were always pictures of you and your brother in the letters. Mostly of you though, with your dog and your kittens, and later your horses. Doc bragged about you a lot, and I guess I feel like I've known you a long time, even though we just met in person lately."

"Wow, I never knew Doc did that. How did he meet your grandpa?" She bent and retrieved the cutlery from the floor.

"From what I can gather, my grandpa was sweet on Mary about the same time Doc started courting her. Doc won, but Grandpa married one of Mary's best friends." His grin was mischievous.

"Your gramma is Dolores? Mary always talks about her. In fact I think I've met her a couple of times when she came to visit." Michelle shook her head in disbelief. *Who would have thought?*

"That's my gramma. Sweetest lady on the face of the planet until you cross her; then you better run for your life."

Cale spooned the fluffy eggs unto the plates and set the pan on the back of the stove. Michelle brought coffee and toast to the table and cream from the fridge. The sun burst over the horizon, and rays of red-gold light slanted across the kitchen. Tears formed in her eyes; the scene was so cozy and comfortable, and she wanted to belong here. Not like when she used to dream about mornings shared with Rob in this house. Instead, she was seized with a desperate urge to be part of Cale's life and share quiet moments like this with him.

She wondered briefly if it was just the house and all the years she spent day dreaming about raising Rob's kids here. Her glance rested on Cale who was reading a research paper while shovelling eggs into his mouth. Michelle examined her raging emotions. It wouldn't be fair to start something with this man if he was just a stand-in for an old flame. Thinking of Rob only brought into focus how mistaken she was in her understanding of their relationship. In retrospect, she was the one always forgiving and understanding, believing him when he said he was sorry, and it would never happen again. Rob never really wanted to settle down to ranching. That was her dream, and he only indulged it because it was easier than fighting about it. Why could she see it so clearly now? It would have saved a world of heartache if she realized it sooner.

Returning her attention to the food on her plate, an image of a dark-haired boy pelting her with horse turds swam to the forefront of her thought. She hadn't thought of that incident in years. It was the summer she was eleven and working at her first paying job, cleaning out Doc's barns. There was something familiar about the kid. She concentrated on the face trying to place him. Setting her fork on the table, she turned her gaze to the man across from her.

"Did you ever visit Doc when you were a kid?"

"Once or twice."

Michelle grinned at the red flush creeping up his face. *I'm right. It was him, the rat bastard. It took me three washings to get the stain out of my shirt.* She pretended not to see the veiled look he gave her over the rim of his cup. Better to let him sweat it out for a bit and see if he'd confess all by his own self. The man seemed to be awfully interested in reading the research papers. Her curiosity got the better of her though, and she poked his shin with her toe.

"Were you the kid who threw horse poop at me in Doc's barn one summer?"

"Busted. I was hoping you wouldn't remember that and put two and two together." A mischievous smile lit his dark eyes.

"You were a horrid little brat. Refused to talk to me and dumped wet poop on me every chance you got. What was wrong with you?" Laughter lightened the tone of her words.

"I had a horrible crush on you, and that was the only way I could think of to get your attention. You spent every spare minute chasing after that older guy who wouldn't give you the time of day."

"I did not," she protested while avoiding his gaze.

"Did to." Cale mimicked her childish tone.

"You might think my feelings for you are too strong for this early in a relationship. Think about it, Michelle. I've loved you for a long time." He captured her fingers and caressed them.

"You don't even know me. That little escapade when I was eleven doesn't count. You can't have lasting feelings based on a crush when you were a kid."

Michelle pulled her fingers free and gathered the dishes as she rose. Her face was burning and unsettling emotions rolled through her. *I trusted Rob and look where that got me. How can I truly believe Cale's feelings are real? I mean it's based on a crush from when he was a kid, but he's right about one thing for sure. I never noticed him, other than the shit slinging. I don't think I ever looked at any other guy except Rob.*

"I'm gonna go start the truck and let it warm up."

His chair scraped on the floor as he stood up. He dropped a kiss on her cheek on the way to get his coat and involuntarily she leaned into his embrace.

"No pressure, Michelle. Just let it happen, give us a chance, okay?"

He was gone before she could answer. Smiling in spite of herself, Michelle went to collect the puppies from the bedroom. Storm was lying in the middle of Cale's bed fast asleep. The dog lifted her head at the yapping of the puppies as Michelle entered the room. With a guilty look, the black dog slid off the bed and moved toward her puppies. Michelle ran her hand over the dog's head to reassure her and bent down to scoop the squirming little dogs into her arms. Holding the wriggling mass carefully, she went to the kitchen and put them in the kennel. Clipping a lead onto Storm's collar, she left the dog by the kennel and fetched her coat and boots.

"Ready to go, when you are," she informed Cale when he returned from outside.

"I fed the horses and checked on the chickens. No eggs yet this morning."

"Thanks for doing chores for me."

"Anytime."

Cale took the kennel out to the truck and stowed it on the back seat. Michelle followed with Storm. The drive into town was silent. The black dog sat in the middle of the seat and surveyed the passing landscape. When they pulled into Doc's yard, Cale reached over and squeezed her hand.

"She'll be fine; don't worry. She's got the two best surgeons around." He attempted to reassure her.

She gave the dog a hug and handed the leash to Cale. Without speaking, Michelle stepped out of the truck and pulled the kennel from the back seat. She wrestled the heavy crate up the walk to Mary's back door while Cale took Storm to the surgery. Reaching the entryway, she rested the container against the jamb and used her foot to knock. Mary opened the door and stepped out of her way.

"Did Cale take Storm over to Luke already?" She peered out the door to satisfy her curiosity.

"Yeah, I don't want to know until it's over."

Placing the kennel on the floor, she released the catch and let the hatch swing out. A rolling mass of black fur emerged onto the kitchen floor. The puppies' fat bellies made it difficult for them to manoeuvre on the slippery floor. Their short thick legs pushed them across the tiles as if they were swimming.

"Cute little tykes, they are," Mary remarked.

She stepped over the wriggling bodies and poured coffee for herself and Michelle. Returning to the table, she plunked down in a chair and fixed her young friend with a stern gaze.

"Now, what's this nonsense I hear about you moving out of the ranch and hightailing it to parts unknown?"

"George knows exactly where I am, or he should if his little blonde remembered to tell him." She knew her defence sounded childish and defensive.

"Can't you two work something out? After all the work you've put in out there, you should be entitled to half the profits."

"You know George... It's his way or the highway. I'm tired of playing that game. If he wants to be the big man and call all the shots, let him deal with the water freezing and the calves coming in the middle of a blizzard." Michelle ran her hand through her hair in exasperation. "I'm tired, Mary. I can't keep doing it alone, and now he wants me to babysit his latest woman."

"Maybe this girl is the one for George," Mary said optimistically.

"Maybe pigs will grow wings and fly."

"Where are you staying? I know you took the horses, because your brother was by here yesterday evening looking for you."

Michelle bent over and picked up a puppy, cuddling it on her lap. There was no use trying to sidetrack the older woman, but contrariness made her hesitate before she answered.

"I'm staying with Cale. He offered me space in the barn for the mares, and the chicken shed was empty, so my hens are in there now."

"Are you sure that's a wise move, Chelly? Cale isn't Rob."

"Thank God for that! Cale actually seems to care what I'm thinking and is willing to help me out. Rob was always too busy expecting me to take care of him all the time."

"You're not going after Cale just because he owns the ranch you've always thought of as yours?"

"It's got nothing to do with that, Mary. Honest. You know I didn't like the man before I met him, which was pretty unfair of me, I guess. I don't like the idea of someone taking over for Doc. There's been too much change lately, and I hate change." Michelle paused, watching the coffee swirl in her mug while she rolled it between her palms. "There's something about Cale... I don't know. He makes me feel safe, listens when I talk, and...I guess I've just never felt like this before."

She raised her head to meet Mary's gaze. A small smile softened the woman's features. She reached across the table and took Michelle's hand in hers.

"I think you're finally growing up, missy. Figuring out what's important in a relationship. It's more than how he fills out his jeans."

"But it helps when he fills them out so well, doesn't it?" Michelle giggled, and Mary joined her.

The puppies set up a racket in the kennel when they woke up from their nap and found no Storm to provide them with lunch. Mary got her trusted milk replacer formula from the fridge and warmed a portion in a bowl. Michelle filled one of the small baby bottles and settled a puppy on her lap where she offered it the nipple. After initially spitting it out, the puppy latched on when she squirted a few drops of liquid on his tongue. Mary picked up another baby and followed the same procedure. The remaining four pups howled their protest making any conversation impossible. Finally, the last of the little black dogs slurped their lunch while their already full siblings rolled on the floor. They were just big enough to start to play a bit; tiny barks sounded in response to sharp little teeth chewing on tails or ears.

"These little heathens will keep you hopping the next few weeks."

Mary set the last puppy on the floor where it waddled over to its litter mates and plopped down at the edge of the heap of bodies.

"I hope they don't keep Cale's parents awake when they come."

Michelle picked the two cups off the table and moved to the counter to refill them. She stepped over the pile of puppies with the full cups balanced carefully and grinned at Mary as she sat opposite her.

"Oh, are his parents coming soon?"

"On the thirtieth. They want to see the place and spend New Year's at the ranch."

"Are you staying while they're here?"

"I wasn't going to. I thought I'd just get a room at the Bluebird for a few days."

"Cale convinced you to stay and meet his mom and dad, did he?"

"Yeah, he said I should stay put, and his mom would like to meet me. Do you think that's kind of weird?"

"I think that boy knows what he wants, and he's out to get it, is what I think." Mary's eyes crinkled mischievously at the corners.

"Shut up! It's not like that at all. He's just doing a neighbour a favour is all." Michelle felt pushed to protest. If she admitted anything else, Mary would have the gossip grapevine flaming the minute she was alone.

"That's not the way I see it, missy. The boy has it bad for you, and you could do a lot worse than Cale Benjamin."

"I never said he wasn't nice. Well, okay, not lately anyway, not since I got to know him when he looked after Storm that night it snowed so badly."

"So....what do you think of him now you know him better?"

"Huh, you just want to know so you can make sure you win the "Who Will Michelle End

Up With Pool". Don't think I haven't heard about the bet you and your cronies have going." She waved a finger at Mary's expression of injured innocence.

"I should have known you never miss a trick. Well, give an old lady a break would you? I put my money on Cale. Am I gonna have to eat crow?"

"If I knew, I'd tell you, believe me. There's something about him I really like him. He's fun to be with... I think it's me I don't trust. Look at all those years I deluded myself Rob was my one and only, and there was never going to be anyone else. I can't make myself trust what I'm feeling. What if I'm wrong again?"

"You've grown up a lot in the last little while, honey. Trust your heart. Don't throw away something strong and right because you're afraid." Mary reached over and squeezed her fingers gently.

"I suppose you're right. I'll just wait and see how things go from here."

The door from the surgery swung open, and Doc and Cale entered the kitchen. Both men pulled the top of their scrubs off and put them in the clinic laundry basket. Michelle's eyes were drawn to Cale's wide shoulders which tapered to his trim waist and the thin line of dark hair disappearing under the band of his scrub pants. She glanced at Mary when she felt a kick on her shin under the table. The woman wore a smug look on her face and raised her eyebrows at Michelle. The heat flared up her neck and into her face, Michelle was acutely aware her face must be fire engine red, and she frowned at Mary in mock irritation. Honestly, the woman was such a tease, and she never quit matchmaking for a second. When she turned back, the men were buttoning their shirts and speaking quietly.

"Well, that went better than expected. We saved most of her leg above the knee." Cale lowered his long frame into the chair beside Michelle and casually rested his arm along the back of her chair.

"Is she going to be okay though…the stump should heal for her?" Michelle kept her gaze on Cale and ignored the looks exchanged between Doc and Mary which she caught in her peripheral vision.

"We had to amputate above the wound. The flesh was avascular, and it wasn't going to heal. It was starting to be necrotic, and pretty soon gangrene would have set in. If the infection went systemic, there's not a whole lot we could do." Doc rubbed his face with his hands after he answered her.

"Luke, are you feeling all right?" Mary frowned at her husband, and Michelle picked up on the worry in her voice.

"I'm fine woman. Just gettin' too old to spend three hours standin' in the surgery anymore."

"Do you want something to eat, a sandwich or…" Michelle started to get to her feet.

"No thanks, Chelly. I think I will go have me a bit of a lie down, though."

The older vet got to his feet and moved toward the stairs. Mary threw a worried glance at the pair by the table before following him out of the room.

"I just can't get used to Doc being old. He's always seemed so…well the same, you know. I thought he was old when I was a kid, but he wasn't really, and now I guess I just can't think of him not being able to do everything he used to." She leaned her head against Cale's arm on her chair back.

"That's why he offered me a partnership in the practice and the option to buy it when he's ready to retire."

"I think maybe it's why I resented you so much before I met you. I didn't want to admit Doc needed help, and it meant things were going to change. I'm tired of change."

"Sometimes change is a good thing, Michelle."

"So far that hasn't been the case for me." She turned her head to look at him while his fingers massaged the nape of her neck under her hair. "Mmm, that feels good."

"Are you willing to give it a chance?"

For a moment, she wasn't sure what to say. The color of his eyes seemed to darken while she hesitated, and she felt the tension in his fingers on her skin.

"I think maybe I am."

The expression of relief that raced across his face made her heart leap in her chest. She reached out and trailed her hand down the side of his face and cupped his cheek in her hand. Cale turned his head and pressed his lips into her palm. She jumped guiltily as Mary entered the kitchen with a frown on her face.

"Is Doc okay?" Michelle moved to meet the older woman and give her a hug.

"I expect he'll be right as rain once he rests a bit. Stubborn old mule, he says he'll slow down, but he never does."

"I'll try to take over as much as I can, and the locum will be here this afternoon. If there are any emergency calls before she arrives call me, and let Doc rest."

Cale got up from the table and stretched his arms over his head. Somehow Michelle forgot to breathe at the sight but managed to not let Mary catch her ogling the man again.

"We should get these monsters out of here before they start screaming again."

She scooped the sleepy pups into the kennel and started to lift it from the floor.

"Here, let me take that out to the truck. You and Mary say your goodbyes, and I'll check on Storm and tell the tech to call me if there are any complications."

At the sound of Mary's chuckle, Michelle dragged her gaze away from the captivating sight of his jean-clad butt. The door to the clinic swung shut behind Cale before she pivoted to meet the older woman's scrutiny. A flush of heat warmed her cheeks, and involuntarily, a guilty smile twitched across her lips.

"A girl can look," she said defensively.

"I don't know, missy, it appears to me you're thinking of doing more than looking."

"Mary!"

She grabbed a tea towel from the back of a chair and threw it at the laughing woman. Mary caught the cloth deftly, folded it neatly, and set it on the counter. Her face sobered when she turned back to Michelle, her blue eyes clouding briefly.

"He's a good man, girl. You could do a lot worse than Cale Benjamin."

"So you said before, Mary. You're right; I admit that. He's been real good to me since he moved into Chetwynd's, and he really didn't have to bother with me at all."

"You think about what I said. That boy really likes you, even though you behaved like a spoilt brat to him."

"What if I'm wrong again? I can't go through all the crap I did after Rob dumped me. I don't trust my own judgement when it comes to my love life."

"You trust Doc don't you?"

"You know I do."

"Well, Doc thinks the boy is the salt of the earth, and he wouldn't be selling this practice to just any Tom, Dick, or Harry. He loves this place, and his clients are his friends. It took him a long time to find the right man to take over."

"Maybe you're right. He makes me feel things I never did with Rob, like we're partners almost, even though I haven't known him very long."

"I met Luke on my twentieth birthday, and we got married the following June. I've never regretted a day. Love isn't based on how long you know someone; it's more about how he makes you feel. No matter how angry I got at Luke over the years, it was never enough for me to ever imagine my life without him in it."

Michelle hugged the older woman and wiped a tear from Mary's cheek. A horn sounded in the yard, and she released her with a smile."Doc will be fine; you just make him rest. Promise. I've gotta go; Cale's waiting. You call us if you need anything at all, and thanks for the advice."

She moved briskly to the door and slipped through quickly to stop the cold air from entering. The snow squeaked under her boots, and suddenly she wanted to laugh and drop in the white powder and make snow angels. She hadn't done that since she was a kid. Giggling at the train of thought, she hurried down the walk and stepped into the warm cab of the pickup.

"Storm is doing great. I left orders for buprenorphine and some NSAIDs for inflammation. She's sleeping right now. The locum called, and she's on her way. I just gave her directions to the house from the highway. I brought some extra milk replacer from the clinic. I'll need to make some more next time

I'm in." Cale reached across and captured her hand, lacing his fingers with hers. With a grin, she slid across the seat and nestled beside him. Nothing in her relationship with Rob ever felt this comfortable or safe; a girl could get used to feeling this way.

"You look happy, any particular reason?" He lifted an eyebrow quizzically before reversing out of the yard and setting off down the snowy road.

"I am happy…happier than I've felt in a long time. I feel like I've finally come home." Her voice came out soft and vibrated with the emotions bubbling in her chest.

"Home with me?" The man didn't take his eyes from the road though she sensed the hope behind his words.

"Yeah, home with you, me, and Storm," she said confidently.

Suddenly she was no longer afraid to open her heart. Doc trusted him. She had never known the man to be wrong in his judgement of people. Truth be told, her own common sense was saying the same thing, and it was darn well about time she listened.

## Chapter Fifteen

Snowy prairie reflected the silver of the full moon, demanding Michelle's attention when she padded across the floor to shrug on her robe and go down to start a pot of coffee. She moved to the window and allowed the magic of moonlight on snow to fill her with a deep sense of peace. Tomorrow Cale's parents were arriving, and there was still a lot to do before they got here. For the moment though, there was time to watch the darkness deepen and then begin to fade, as the scales of light tipped in favour of the morning. Only a short while after the solstice, and already the hours of light were growing perceptibly longer each day.

The morning star paled against the brightening blue of the sky; the sun swung free, climbing the heavens on chains of gold. Long red-gold rays slanted over the undulating landscape, throwing the small depressions into bluish shadows and touching the rolling land with a blush of rose. A high whinny broke the stillness and shook her from the contemplation of the winter sunrise.

Michelle hastened down to the kitchen and set the coffee to brew. Grabbing her barn coat from the chair and shoving her feet into her boots, she left the house and crunched across the yard to the barn. It took only a few minutes to check the water and throw some flakes of hay into the corral before turning the horses out. A quick stop at the hen house on the way back to the house produced enough eggs for breakfast and to take in to Mary. Bucket of eggs in hand, she hurried toward the warmth of the house.

Shedding the outdoor gear in the mudroom, she pushed the inner door open and entered the kitchen. Cale stood at the counter, pouring coffee into two mugs; his hair was mused, and his loose flannel pants stopped just above his hip bones. A rush of heat which had nothing to do with the temperature in the room enveloped her. Dear God, the man was good to look at. He moved across to the table, favouring her with a heart-stopping smile on the way.

"Morning." She found her voice.

"Looks like it's gonna be a nice day." His voice was still husky with sleep.

"The sunrise was beautiful."

"Better from my room. The one you're in faces north, not east."

"When can Storm come home?" Michelle changed the subject quickly from the more dangerous direction his comment was headed.

"If all goes well, we can bring her home today, as long as we watch her closely and keep her medicated for the pain."

His grin melted her heart and made her forget what she was about to say. In an effort to hide the confusion, she picked up her mug and sat at the table to savour it. Cale swallowed his in two gulps and went back to the pot. Running water in the sink, he set about washing the eggs and laying them on a tea towel to drip dry.

"Do you want to eat here, or should we just run into Doc's with these and fix breakfast there?"

He dried his hands and returned to the table with his coffee. Michelle looked up with a start as his shadow fell across her face. He leaned down and kissed her gently on the lips and ran a hand over her head, picking a piece of hay out of her hair as he did so.

"I knew there was something I forgot to do this morning. All taken care of now." He teased tapping her nose with the stalk of timothy hay.

Michelle slapped his hand away and stood quickly to cover her confusion. It unsettled her that he could affect her so much just by touching her. The relationship was so different from what she experienced with Rob. Cale drew her to him like a compass needle to true north. The intensity was frightening. It was already hard to think about her life without his presence in it, which in her opinion was very dangerous. It wouldn't be easy to cope if things fell apart. Although there really wasn't anything to fall apart yet, was there?

"Earth to Michelle." Cale waved a hand in front of her eyes. "Breakfast here or at the clinic?'

"At the clinic, I guess. The sooner we collect Storm and get her home, the sooner I can clean this place up before your mom gets here."

"The puppies are quiet. Did you feed them already this morning?"

"This morning and three times last night," she said wryly.

"Good. I'll load them in the truck. You bring the eggs, and we're off."

"Huh, Mr. Cheerful. Where were you last night when they were squawking?"

"I'll take puppy duty tonight if you want...or we could share it?" He waggled his eyebrows and gave her a seductive smile.

"Share it how?"

"You, me, the puppies, my room, one bed?"

The look on his face sent her into gales of laughter which only increased as it changed to one of affronted pride.

"My best line and you laugh? Who can resist an offer like that?"

Still laughing, she collected the eggs from the counter and went out to the truck, leaving him to trail behind and wrestle with the puppy crate and the door. He joined her in short order, grinning happily.

"What are you so happy about, Lothario?"

"You laughed, but you didn't say no. Hope springs eternal..."

"You wish!"

* * * *

The kitchen door swung open while Michelle still had one foot on the step. Mary moved out of the way to allow entrance. Cale came in behind with the crate of puppies and placed it on the floor. Michelle gave Mary a quick hug and scanned the room for Doc. Not seeing him, she released the older woman and ventured into the living room.

"Doc's over at Harvey's. I told him he couldn't go into the clinic, so he went to have coffee and complain about getting old."

"Is he feeling better this morning?" Michelle came back into the kitchen.

"Some. Still a little grey around the gills, but not so tired."

"I'm gonna go check on our patient and see if the locum needs anything," Cale said before leaving the room.

The puppies set up a racket as the sound of the door closing woke them. Michelle moved to the crate and opened the hatch. Six bundles of black fur came scrambling out complaining loudly about the empty state of their bellies. Laughing, the two women each picked up a puppy and collected a bottle of supplement from the fridge. Mary warmed the milk, and soon the puppies were slurping happily. The remaining four continued to scream at the top of their lungs. Holding the puppy and bottle with one hand, Michelle poured some milk into a shallow bowl and set it on the floor. The little creatures converged on it, crawling through it and sneezing when it got up their noses. They ceased their shrill squealing as some of the milk got into their mouths, and they contented themselves with capturing as much of the fluid as they could from the floor and their fur.

Soon the puppies were all fed and after a short bout of playtime, fell asleep in a heap beside their kennel. The sound of footsteps in the hall leading to the clinic drew Michelle's attention from the small dogs. She raised her gaze as the door swung open, and Storm hopped into view. The dog was a little wobbly on her three good legs although she moved with more ease than she had with her injured leg still present.

Slipping to her knees, Michelle held her arms out, and the black dog made her way across the floor and sat on her haunches in front of her. Gently, she stroked the soft black fur on the dog's head. Storm rewarded her with a huge sloppy kiss before gingerly lying down with a sigh. Cale followed Storm into the kitchen and poured himself a mug of coffee.

"How does her stump look?" Michelle rose to her feet, careful not to disturb Storm.

"It looks good. We can take her home with us if you like."

Before she could answer, the door swung open again, and a tall woman with flaming red hair entered the room. Michelle closed her mouth with a snap. *This is the locum? The woman is drop dead gorgeous. I wonder if Doc or Cale hired her?*

"Hey, Carrie. This is Michelle, a family friend of Doc and Mary's. I don't think you guys have met have you?" Cale introduced the woman without batting an eye.

"Hi, Michelle. I've heard lots of good things about you. I'm pleased to meet you." Carrie crossed the room and held her hand out.

"Hi, Carrie. Nice to meet you, too."

"Coffee?" Mary offered.

"Don't mind if I do. I have a bit of a break before the next client is due." The locum checked her watch before taking a chair at the table.

"Has it been busy?' Michelle attempted to ignore the fact the woman was beautiful and should not be allowed anywhere near Cale. She would behave like a grownup, she promised herself. *Cale is not Rob. He's not going to go play with her and then come expecting me to act like nothing happened.*

"Not too bad, no emergencies yet." Carrie smiled over the rim of the coffee cup, the corners of her iridescent green eyes crinkling with amusement.

"Good to hear," Cale remarked. He bent down and ruffled the top of Storm's head. "We should get this girl home and settled. Are you ready to go, Michelle?"

"Sure, I'll pack up the little mutts, and we're ready to roll."

In short order, the puppies were in the truck, and Michelle waited while Storm came carefully down the snowy walk. The dog paused periodically to lean a shoulder against Cale's leg for support. Half way to the truck, the vet stooped down, gently gathered the dog into his arms and carried her the remainder of the way. Once in the cab, the big dog ensconced herself in the middle of the seat and leaned against the back rest looking very satisfied with herself. Michelle climbed in beside her and heard Cale laugh as he went around to the driver's side and got in.

The ride home was quiet. Michelle forced the image of the locum's face from her mind. Cale was here with her, and they were going home together. He hadn't been more than friendly to the woman. Trust was a hard thing to believe in after the lessons Rob taught her, but her heart said Cale was different, and he certainly never behaved like Rob did.

"Did you know Carrie before she came here?" The words came out before she could stop them.

"She was three years behind me at WCVM. I knew who she was, but I've never really seen her much." Cale shifted his gaze from the road to give her a puzzled look.

"So Doc hired her?"

"Yeah, he asked me what I knew about her, and everything I heard was good, so I told him that. Why, is it important?"

"I guess not, I don't know…" Her voice trailed off, and she was annoyed to feel tears building in her eyes.

Cale stomped on the brake, stopping the truck in the middle of the range road near the ranch. He reached across the seat and took her chin in his fingers. He gently turned her face toward him, and she met his gaze. The tears in her eyes gave his features a blurry outline, and it was hard to read his expression.

"Michelle, look at me. I am not your stupid ex-whatever. I am not going to run off with any woman except you. Understand? Only you."

His fingers tightened on her jaw for a moment and then released her. The vehicle moved forward, and she surreptitiously wiped the tears from her cheeks.

"I don't mean to keep comparing you to Rob. I really don't. I guess I just don't get why a guy would want to be with someone like me when there's a gorgeous female around."

"I think you're the most beautiful woman I've ever seen, so I can't agree with your logic."

Although his tone was light, the knuckles on his hands were white as he gripped the wheel. She reached across Storm and covered his right hand with her own and squeezed gently.

"You're pretty hot yourself, for a fancy horse vet."

Cale rewarded her with a smile which took her breath away. She returned her hand to her lap and smiled.

## Chapter Sixteen

Michelle finished chores and headed to the house, carefully tucking three eggs in her jacket pocket. There always seemed to be one or two hens who laid their eggs late in the day. The door to the mudroom burst open as she reached the porch, and Cale emerged shrugging into his coat.

"Emergency, gotta go. Storm and the crew are in the kitchen. Don't know when I'll be back." He paused on the way past to plant a kiss on her nose. "Keep the home fires burning." He grinned as he leaped into his vehicle and drove off kicking snowy gravel from his tires.

"Don't forget to put your seat belt on," she called after the departing truck. "God, I sound like his mother."

Continuing into the house, she washed up, fed the puppies, checked on Storm, and spent the next three hours cleaning the house. It had been quite a while since the old house was given a good cleaning. Michelle wiped last summer's fly blow off the window and door frames and polished the inside panes of the windows. Standing back to admire her hand work, she was only marginally pleased with the result of three hours of hard work. Nothing except a coat of fresh paint was going to help the woodwork, and there wasn't anything she could do about the worn spots on the kitchen floor.

"Well, Storm, at least it looks better than when I started."

The short late December daylight was fading, and she flicked on the overhead light in the room. A glance at the clock on the stove told her it was quarter to five in the afternoon. From the corner of her eye, Michelle caught the flash of headlights as a truck turned into the yard.

"Cale's home," she sang the words to Storm.

A truck door slammed followed by footsteps and a soft knock on the outer door. Frowning, Michelle crossed the room and stepped into the dark mudroom, turning on the light as she moved to the door. Pulling the door open, she controlled her surprise at the sight of Kayla standing in the illumination thrown by porch light.

"Hi, Kayla. What are you doing here? Oh, come on in, seeing as you're here," she said more than a little ungraciously.

"I don't mean to bother you…I just didn't know where else to go…" The woman's voice trailed off before she burst into tears.

"Oh for mercy's sake, come in and tell me what the jackass did this time."

"It's not his fault." The anxious woman ventured carefully past Michelle, who took her coat and hung it on a peg, indicating she should leave her boots by the door.

"It never is," Michelle said dryly.

Swiftly, she poured two cups of coffee and set them on the table. Kayla hovered just inside the kitchen door, looking like she was ready to bolt at any second. Storm hopped over and pushed her head into the distraught woman's hand, either offering comfort or mooching for a pet, Michelle wasn't sure which. The contact seemed to break the woman's concentration on her thoughts, and she moved to sit across from Michelle. She was silent for a few moments, brushing the tears from her face before she looked at Michelle.

"I thought I'd find him here..." Kayla spoke so softly it was hard to understand the words.

"Find who, Cale? Is something wrong with one of the horses?"

"No, Rob. I thought Rob would be here." Her face flamed bright red as she spoke.

"This is probably the last place he would come. Did you guys have a fight or something?"

"Sort of. He wants to start a family right away, and I want to wait until next year. I've already given up some valuable training time with my horse, and I need to start working to get ready for the spring shows. I didn't go to Tucson so I could spend time with Rob and set up house, but all he wants to do is live in that old trailer and party."

"Sounds like the Rob I know, well except for the babies part."

"You didn't talk about starting a family when you were…" Her voice trailed off, and if possible, the red in her cheeks deepened.

"Engaged, you mean. Like when you met him and married him." Michelle fought to keep the angry edge from her tone.

"I didn't know he was engaged. He never mentioned it until after we were married in Vegas. It was too late to have second thoughts by then and…besides I love him." Kayla defended herself.

"So, you had a fight, you came looking for him here, and he's obviously not here. Maybe you should leave now." Michelle got to her feet abruptly and took her coffee cup to the sink.

"Michelle, I really need to talk to you. You've known him your whole life. I'm still trying to figure out what makes him tick."

"When you find that out, let me know."

"He didn't want to have kids with you?" the woman persisted.

"No he didn't." The words exploded from her before she could stop them. "He wanted to rodeo and party, and he wanted a pretty fiancée on his arm when it was convenient, like when sponsors were around. Made him look stable and responsible and all that."

"So why is he so insistent we start trying to get pregnant so quickly? I don't understand."

"Got me, maybe he really does love you and thinks it's a good way to tie you to him. Don't get me wrong, Rob loves kids, and he's good with them. He just didn't want any of ours running around." To her surprise, the sharp knife of pain which usually accompanied this train of thought was curiously absent. Unbidden, Cale's face flashed across her inner eye.

"I'm sorry, Michelle. I shouldn't have come here. All I seem to do is cause you more pain and embarrassment." Kayla got to her feet and moved toward the mud room.

"Wait, Kayla. It's old news, water under the bridge. Rob made his choice, he married you. That's something I could never get him to commit to. It took the combined efforts of me, his mom, and Mary, just to get him to propose to me. I guess I should have known better, but he was like a habit. For as long as I can remember, everyone assumed we would get married and combine the two properties. I think Rob was afraid to go against the grain and instead just kept procrastinating. There was always something. This rodeo, that rodeo, CFR, NFR, he couldn't find the time."

"Do you think he married me on an impulse and because he was drunk?" Tears threatened to spill from the luminous blue eyes.

Michelle took a minute to marshal her thoughts and choose the words carefully. The woman seemed to be sincere in her feelings for Rob. And for all the reasons she was angry with the man notwithstanding, he was still her friend, and she wanted him to be happy. Only it was supposed to be her he was happy with. A tiny smile crossed her face.

"Maybe a tiny bit, Kayla. Rob is no fool though. He can drink most cowboys under the table and still put in a good ride, so he knew what he was doing. The booze might have given him the courage to actually take the big step, but he must love you, or he would never have married you. He's not an easy man to live with. His daddy expected a lot from him, and nothing he ever did was good enough. It's almost like he's punishing himself for not being some superman his dad wanted him to be. You know, I never actually figured that out until just now."

"You think I should give in and give up my dreams to make him happy?" A single tear slid down her face.

"Not hardly! You go find the man, drag him out of whatever bar you find him in. Don't listen to any excuses. Take him home, sit him down, and work it out between you. He has dreams, big deal, so do you. I gave up going to college because I didn't want to be away from him, worst mistake of my life. Tell him your dreams are important, too, and if he loves you like he says he does, you'll work it out."

"Really? You think he'll be willing to compromise?" The blonde's expression brightened considerably.

"He will if you stand your ground. Rob's as hard headed as the worst of them, but underneath, he's a big old softie. Remember that when you're so mad you could take a bull whip to him, and you'll get your way every time. He never looked at me the way he looks at you. He thinks you hung the moon and the sun rises out of your backside. Go get him and drag him on home."

"Thanks, Michelle. I'm sorry I bothered you with all this. I didn't know who to talk to, and Mary suggested I come and see you. Oops, I promised not to tell you that part..." Kayla smothered a laugh with her hand.

"Ah, Miss Mary. I should have seen her hand in this. Driving home the point you and Rob are married and talking about babies, hoping I'll open my eyes and see the great guy who is interested in me." Michelle let a giggle escape her lips and suddenly both women were laughing.

"Thank you so much. I'll let you know how it goes."

Kayla surprised her by giving her by giving a huge bear hug and a large smile. After a moment's hesitation, she hugged her back and wiped the last of the tear smudges from the other woman's cheeks.

"Go get Rob, woman, go." She gave the blonde a gentle push toward the door.

She stood in the window and watched the truck lights bounce as the vehicle drove down the rutted land. *Bye, Rob*. The thought took her off guard, and suddenly, everything was okay in her world. Storm was alive and getting better, four puppies were spoken for, and Cale would be home when he finished at the clinic. She would never have to worry if he was in some bar with a buckle bunny on his lap, or off doing

Lord only knew what stupid stunt because someone dared him. *Idiot.*

Michelle turned on the radio and sang along with The Travelling Mabels latest hit while she tidied the kitchen. The humour in Eva's lyrics made her smile more than once before she was done with her tasks. A yawn made her wonder what time it was. It didn't seem possible it was ten p.m. already. She carried the puppies into Cale's bedroom after feeding them and laughed to find Storm already curled up on the bed where the puppies couldn't reach her. The thought of traipsing up the cold stairs was uninviting, and she decided to keep Storm company and watch the early news.

Quickly stripping off her jeans and sweater, she deposited them on a chair and grabbed one of Cale's thick flannel shirts. She found the remote under a pillow and settled under the warm duvet with the big black dog curled into her side. She lowered the volume to almost nothing so the sleeping babies would stay that way and snuggled deeper into the cozy nest of pillows and covers. *Cale's parents get here tomorrow. At least the house is clean.* The thought was the last thing which drifted through her mind before the television screen blurred, and her eyes shut.

Storm's soft whine woke her, and she tried to focus her eyes. The red numbers on the clock read 1:00 a.m. Her mind registered the time a second before the mattress dipped, and she heard Cale's weary sigh. She moved to get out

228

of his bed and go upstairs. Before she did more than push back the duvet, his arm encircled her waist and pulled her against his warm body. Her breath stuck in her throat at the touch of his stirring manhood against her back. His lips nuzzled the back of her neck before he exhaled in what sounded like utter contentment.

"Go back to sleep, Chelly. Morning comes early."

The words slurred a bit and trailed off. Suspicion stirred in her and she turned her head and sniffed his breath. Cale smelled of antiseptic and soap, and she was ashamed for thinking it might be otherwise. Never again, she promised herself and relaxed into his embrace.

"Night, Cale," she whispered.

## Chapter Seventeen

Sharp insistent squeals of displeasure roused Michelle from the dark comfort of sleep. She rolled unto her back and pushed ineffectually at the heavy object restricting her movement. Strong fingers closed over her hand, and her eyes flew open. Cale smiled at her, his hair dark against the white pillow. Releasing her hand, he brushed the hair out of her face and drew her toward him. She leaned against his warm chest and enjoyed the wonderful feel of his lips on her skin. He feathered tiny kisses across her cheekbones and over her jaw, sending delicious tendrils of desire shooting through her body where they pooled in her groin. The bedclothes rustled as he pulled her closer so she lay on top of his body, her hips and legs encircled by his strong thighs. She wriggled to get comfortable and smiled at his body's reaction. His kiss deepened, becoming more than a casual good morning when his tongue traced the curve of her lower lip. She all but inhaled it as she gasped at the jolt of desire lancing directly to her centre.

Her tongue danced with his, her nipples tightening and tingling where she rubbed them against the coarse hair of his chest. In a swift maneuver which would have done a steer wrestler proud, Cale flipped her over onto her back still keeping her imprisoned between his thighs. He deserted her mouth to delve his tongue into her ear and suckle gently on the lobe. Her body arched involuntarily toward him when his hand slid down and captured the sensitive flesh of her breast. Gently he stroked and kneaded the pliable mound, tenting his fingers over the peak and stroking upward toward the straining tip but not touching it.

Michelle wrapped her arms around his neck and strained closer, inarticulately begging for his touch. In response, his fingers danced and teased across the pebbled flesh, and his hot mouth covered her lips. His penis twitched and throbbed against the apex of her thighs. The flannel shirt which she hadn't bothered to fasten the night before slipped to the sides pushed out of the way. Her nipples burned for the slick pleasure of his tongue. With a wicked smile, she slipped a hand down over his buttocks and along the side of his hip. His body convulsed against her, and she arched her back higher, presenting the darkened bud of her nipple against his hand.

Her fingers found the warm bobbing head where it pressed on her abdomen, catching the viscous fluid of his pre-cum she traced a fingertip around the straining head. Teasing him as he had teased her, she stroked up the tulip of his penis but didn't wrap her hand around it. His mouth closed over her nipple, and he nipped the rosy tip gently. Forgetting her intention to tease, Michelle smeared the bit of fluid along his shaft and pumped her hand. Cale's hips bucked under her attention, and he moved to place his knee between her legs. His mouth deserted her breast and left wet kisses down her stomach while his talented fingers caressed the hot, wet folds of her labia.

The tip of his tongue touched the swollen bud of womanhood and then gently lapped, swirling the hot steady pressure of his mouth over her clitoris. His hands were busy teasing her tingling nipples and sliding the fingers of his other hand in and out of her vagina which was twitching and contracting around them. Michelle's breath came in gasps as the erotic sensations rolled through her, nothing in the world existed beyond Cale's hands and mouth on her body and the pleasure he was awakening within her.

The feeling of ecstasy was so intense it bordered on painful. She knew the peak was approaching and strained toward the wonderful rush of release. Suddenly, Cale drew her whole clitoral area into his mouth and sucked while driving the hard point of his tongue into the bud. At the same time, the fingers in her vagina reached upward with a tickling motion, and the intense pressure exploded inside her as he stroked her clit from the outside and from within. Before the ripples of pleasure subsided, he lifted her legs over his shoulders and drove himself into her hot and ready body.

Michelle grasped the duvet in her hands and rode the thrusts of his body, matching them with her own, to the towering crescendo of completion.

Cale collapsed beside her and rolled her with him, their bodies still joined.

"How's that for a good morning?" he asked impishly.

"A girl could get used to it," she replied.

The puppies squealed louder, and Storm pushed her nose into the back of Cale's neck, making him jump and roll away from Michelle. Quickly, she swung her feet to the floor and stood up, gathering the flannel shirt around her. Behind her, she heard the rustle of bedclothes as Cale got out of bed as well. She hurried down the hall to the kitchen and got the container of supplement milk from the fridge. Pouring some into a bowl she warmed it in the microwave. Cale entered the room and padded across to the wood stove in his bare feet. The sounds of him stoking the fire created a warm homey feeling in her heart. Storm hopped into view with the six puppies rolling along behind on their short stubby legs. Scooping one up, Michelle crossed to the padded armchair by the stove and settled the puppy on her lap. Cale brought an afghan and tucked it around her bare legs and dropped a kiss on her hair. She looked up with a smile and laughed at his expression as tiny dog teeth closed on his pajama leg and pulled.

"Little heathen," he exclaimed, picking the black ball of fur up and snagging the second bottle of warm milk from the chair beside her.

Storm hopped up unto the old horsehide sofa against the wall to escape her babies' attentions. With a puppy securely in the crook of his arm and the bottle held in his hand so the puppy could eat, Cale fetched a low dish from the counter and filled it with warm milk from the container and dropped a bit of canned puppy food into it. Mashing it with a spoon, he carried it back to the throng of hungry creatures and placed it in front of them.

"Soon, they'll be eating enough on their own, and we won't need to do puppy patrol." Michelle glanced at him and smiled.

"They do grow fast, which is a very good thing in this case. Storm has the right idea, lie on the couch, and let someone else deal with the kids." His vibrant laugh sent shivers of happiness through her.

"What time did I say your are folks getting here?" She didn't want to be half-dressed when they arrived, that was for sure.

"Around two, if I remember right. They'll call when they get to town. I think Mom wants to stop and say hi to Mary before they come out to the ranch."

"That could be dangerous you know," Michelle warned. "You know what a matchmaker Mary is. She'll be putting all sorts of ideas in your mom's head."

"Probably nothing more than she's figured out on her own. I bet Mary and Gramma have been gossiping about us non-stop, and what Gramma knows Mom knows."

Cale set the puppy down on the floor and picked up a milk-soaked litter mate. He snagged an old towel off the pile beside the chair, kept there to wipe down muddy floors and dogs. Expertly, he wrapped the wriggling bundle and offered the nipple to the complaining beast.

"You do that well. Wait 'til it's dirty diapers and screaming kids," she teased him.

"As long as said babies are yours and mine, I'll be there like a dirty shirt." His voice was warm and low.

"Whoa, cowboy, who said anything about you and me having babies?" Her startled gaze flew to his face, and she felt the heat flooding her cheeks at the intimate thought.

"Umm, seems to me we made a good start this morning. Unless you're on the pill, I was too distracted and sleepy to think of using anything when you bushwhacked me." Concern clouded his expression. "Are you...on the pill I mean?"

Michelle shook her head and mentally kicked herself a thousand times for being so stupid. "It didn't agree with me, and well...I guess I was kinda hoping if I got preggers it would push Rob into actually tying the knot. Dumb, I know..." Her voice trailed off.

"No use crying over spilt milk, Chelle. Odds are nothing happened, and if it did..."

"Easy for you to say! You're not the one who has to raise the kid by yourself, not to mention listening to Mary, and God forbid

George, rag on me for getting myself knocked up—"

Her words were cut off abruptly by Cale's lips capturing her mouth. The puppies squirmed between them, but she ignored them caught up in the magic of his kiss. He broke away with a smile and returned to his seat, after depositing the full puppy on the floor and selecting another.

"You won't be raising any kid of mine by yourself. You're putting the cart in front of the horse anyway. I don't think the chances of you being pregnant are very high. Besides which my momma would kick my ass from here to hell and back if I didn't step up and take responsibility for my actions." He grinned at her, his hair falling across his forehead.

"Hummph, so you'd only be there because it was your duty?" Michelle muttered.

"Not hardly, woman. In case you haven't noticed, I like your company, and it would make me very happy to go to bed every night and wake up with you beside me for the rest of our lives." His expression turned serious as he spoke, and his gaze caught and held her own with an intensity she felt in her bones.

"Well, like you said, it's not likely is it?" Michelle set her puppy down and picked up another.

"Even so, Michelle, think about what I said. I'm not just teasing. We make a good team, and you can't deny the sparks fly when we're together. You don't have to be pregnant to get me to marry you."

"Who's getting married?" An unfamiliar female voice cut across Michelle's jumbled thoughts.

"Mom, Dad…" Cale scrambled to his feet, a tide of red sweeping up his face. "I thought you weren't going to be here 'til this afternoon."

"We got on the road early and thought we'd surprise you." Carson Benjamin's voice sounded amused.

"Well, you did do that." Cale set the last puppy on the floor and moved to his mother and hugged her.

"So, I see. Hello, Michelle dear. I know we spoke on the phone, but it's lovely to meet you in person." Peggy Benjamin directed the last of her comment to Michelle.

"It's nice to meet you, Mrs. Benjamin, you too, Mr. Benjamin." She bent and put the sleeping puppy with its littermates.

"My pleasure, Michelle." Carson smiled at her.

"There's coffee in the pot. Help yourself while I get some clothes on, and I'll help you bring stuff in." Cale hurried down the hall toward the bedroom.

*Coward!* Michelle stayed where she was. There was no way she could get up with his parents standing there. For God's sake, she was clad only in a flannel shirt and nothing else but her pelt. She smiled uncertainly at Cale's dad when he moved past her to the coffee pot. Peggy

Benjamin settled herself in the chair her son just vacated and regarded her with an amused look on her face. Michelle cursed silently as she felt her face and neck heat with embarrassment. She didn't need a mirror to know her face was fire engine red. She could look guilty on a good day, and there was no denying the intimacy of her relationship with the woman's son.

Carson brought his wife her coffee and moved away to prowl about the kitchen, looking at the plumbing under the sink and inspecting the fuse box. Peggy observed him with an indulgent expression on her pretty face. She caught Michelle's attention, raised her eyebrows, and smiled. She grinned in return and twisted her head to look at Cale as he re-entered the kitchen.

"What do you think, Dad? It's an old house and a little rundown, but the land is good, and the out buildings aren't in bad shape." He tucked his shirt into his waistband while joining his dad to inspect the pipes in the laundry room.

Whatever Carson replied was lost in the sound of the door closing behind them and the rattle of something metallic. Storm chose that moment to get up and hop over Peggy, shoving her nose into the woman's hand for attention.

"That's Storm. We had to amputate her leg recently. We tried everything, but it wouldn't heal. I think there was too much damage, and we're not sure how long she was hurt before I found her. Which reminds me, I need to get her

238

meds." She stood up wrapping the afghan around her waist and not meeting the older woman's gaze. At least his dad wasn't in the room.

"Yes, Cale told me about her. You took on a lot when you rescued her with everything else you had on your plate. Is there anything I can do to help with her meds?"

"Thanks for the offer. She's a good girl and takes her pills without complaining." Michelle shuffled across the floor, clutching the heavy knitted blanket with one hand.

"Why don't you go get changed, dear? I was young once, too, believe it or not, and I remember how awkward it can be when people show up unexpectedly. I'm sure Storm can wait a few more minutes."

"It's not like that…" Her voice trailed off at the knowing look on Peggy's face.

"Go. Get changed before the men get back from exploring the plumbing." She made a shooing motion with her hand before sliding from her chair to sit on the floor with Storm and the puppies. "I'll hold the fort 'til you get back."

Michelle fled down the hall, fighting to hold back tears. *So much for making a good first impression on his parents. The first time they meet me, I'm sitting there bold as brass, half naked in their son's kitchen.* Quickly, she gathered her clothes off the floor and pulled them on. She was passing through the doorway when Cale and his dad came down the hall toward the stairs. Taking a steadying breath, she stepped into the passage and smiled. Might as well brave it out; it was pretty obvious where she slept last night anyway. No point in making it worse by trying to hide the fact. Besides, she reasoned, they were both consenting adults. Cale interrupted her train of thought by kissing her happily as he went past her. Carson grinned warmly as he passed, his smile a carbon copy of his son's. Her heart lifted, and she grinned on her way back to the kitchen, maybe things would work out okay after all.

Entering the kitchen, she got Storm's pills and extracted a chicken hot dog from the fridge. Stuffing the pills into the meat, she offered the dog a piece without anything secreted in it first, followed by the bit with the pill. The black dog swallowed both, scarcely stopping to chew and looked hopefully for more.

"She really is a sweetheart, isn't she?" Peggy stroked the soft fur on the dog's head.

"Considering what she's been through, yeah she is. I don't think I'd be as forgiving if I was her," Michelle admitted.

"Yes, humans could learn a lot about patience and forgiveness from animals couldn't they? Cale said two of the babies don't have homes yet, is that still the case?"

"We have homes for four of them. Clint, Mary and Doc's neighbour is taking two, and Mrs. Becker spoke for a male. Cale mentioned Mary was interested in one, but the other two are still up for grabs."

"Carson and I were talking it about it on the drive up, and we'd like a little female if there's one left. If not, we'll take a male, gender isn't really that important to us." The woman scooped up a sleepy puppy and laid it across her lap on its back and stroked the fat belly. "Babies are so sweet. Too bad they have to grow up. That's just a mother talking though. When Cale and his brother were growing up, I was counting the days until they would be old enough to get out on their own. Once they're gone, you wish they were little again." Peggy laughed at her own nonsensical thoughts.

"I can believe that. I babysit for my friend Laurie sometimes, and I'm a wreck when I get back from her three kids. They're sweet little things, but oh my stars, they're busy." Michelle found herself laughing and confiding in Cale's mother. "Makes me wish for some of my own sometimes."

"Mary tells me you were engaged to your childhood sweetheart, but it didn't work out." The older woman's tone was gentle.

"Trust Mary. Rob and I grew up together. This was actually his family's ranch. My place is across the coulee. You would have driven by it on your way here. My brother is looking after it now. We're not exactly on speaking terms at the moment, which is why Cale offered to let me stay here."

"Are you sure that's all there is to it, dear? I know my son; living with a woman is not something he would enter into lightly. He's always talking about you when he calls home."

"Your son is a great guy, and we get on really well with each other. Rob and I were friends, and then when we grew up, we were lovers but not really friends anymore, if that makes any sense to you." Michelle frowned while she attempted to marshal her thoughts.

"I know better than you might think Michelle," Peggy said enigmatically.

"With Cale, it's like he's my best friend even though I haven't known him that long, but it's so much more than that as well. He's the sexiest man I've ever seen... Oh my stars, I didn't mean to say that!" Her face felt like it was on fire. This was his mother she was talking to for heaven's sake. What a thing to say.

"Don't be upset. I can tell by the way you look at him when you think no one is watching that you are interested in more than what he looks like. Although, I must say, if we were talking about bloodlines in breeding horses, I'd have to say Carson and I were a good match."

"Peggy, you're gonna scare that girl right out of here talking like that," Carson chided his wife.

"I didn't hear you come down the hall, darling." Peggy favoured him with an amused look.

"I'm sure this young lady doesn't want to hear her boyfriend's mother comparing him to progeny of breeding stock." The tall rangy rancher looked apologetically at Michelle.

"Okay then, changing the subject. Let's bring your things in from the truck, Dad. Chelly, will you show Mom where their room is and see if there's anything they need up there?" Cale moved toward the mudroom and escape, followed by his father.

\* \* \*

The rest of the morning flew by. Michelle and Peggy went over the old ranch house from top to bottom. Pen and paper in hand, they moved from room to room, discussing what needed to be done to spruce the place up. Most of the upstairs bedrooms were in need of paint and new wallpaper along with window dressings. For the most part, the upper floors were wide oak boards in need of refinishing, which could wait 'til summer. The kitchen floor was covered in worn, discoloured linoleum which desperately needed to be pulled up and replaced with tile or laminate. The living room and the parlour had the original hardwood floors which still retained their beauty and could be left for the time being.

Peggy stuck her head into the shower stall of the bathroom off the kitchen and shook her head. The white metal of the walls was discoloured and showing rust stains, and the other fixtures were in no better shape. The laundry room revealed flooring and plumbing which needed immediate replacement and went to the top of the "to do" list.

"We'll take a run into High River or Okotoks tomorrow and pick up most of the things we need to fix the most urgent things on the list," Peggy said, emerging from the laundry room.

"There's a lot to do, are you sure you want to spend your visit with Cale pulling up lino and painting woodwork?" Michelle asked uncertainly.

"That's what we came up for. I didn't know you were here at the house, and Cale isn't one to worry about aesthetics. As long as things are still working, it doesn't matter to him what it looks like."

"True, although he's way tidier than my brother, thank goodness."

"You ladies ready for some dinner?" Carson Benjamin stepped through the mudroom door followed by his son.

"That would be lovely. What's in the freezer, Cale?" His mother smiled and patted her son on the cheek.

"A tray of Mary's lasagne, some buffalo roasts, and maybe some French fries," he answered her.

"Now, Peggy, this is our first night here. Let's go into town and celebrate Cale's new job and his new home." Carson made a funny face, and Michelle giggled.

"Don't encourage the man for heaven's sake," Peggy said in mock annoyance. "He'll start doing his impressions if you give an ounce of encouragement."

"Dinner out is a great idea, Dad. Let's go to the steak house in Longview. They have the best food anywhere around here." Cale said.

"Sounds like a plan. We'll take our truck if you don't mind." Carson shrugged into his coat and pointed his key fob toward the red vehicle outside which roared into life.

In short order, Storm and the puppies were cared for and safely situated. Michelle settled in the rear seat of the quad cab. Cale joined her, capturing her fingers in his after the seat belts were fastened. A warm feeling of happiness swept over her. For the first time in longer than she remembered, it felt like she was part of a family. It was definitely a very nice feeling.

The ride into town was short, and before long, they were seated in the tiny dining room of the steak house. The restaurant had a cozy comfortable ambiance, and the conversation flowed easily. Michelle found herself laughing at Carson and Peggy as they kibitzed and teased each other. She met Cale's warm gaze across the table. For a moment, it seemed there was no one else in the world but the two of them. He reached across the white tablecloth and took her hand in his. A smile of pure happiness blossomed within her chest and spread across her face. Nothing in her whole life ever felt this right. A wonderful sense of belonging enveloped her.

"Hey you two, if you keep looking at each other like that, you'll melt the candles," Peggy teased.

Michelle withdrew her hand as she experienced a rush of heat across her face. Cale laughed and recaptured her fingers. He raised her hand to his lips and brushed a kiss across her knuckles. The intimate gesture sent thrills of pleasure spiralling through her stomach, and she trembled.

"Isn't that sweet, Carson? I remember when we were at that stage in our relationship." Peggy's eyes were shiny with tears.

Michelle heard the words and thought briefly about telling her they were just friends. Honesty quieted her tongue as she acknowledged what she was feeling was a lot more than friendship. Cale took the situation in hand, picking up his beer without taking his gaze from her face.

"Let's toast shall we? To the woman I love, my new job, and my new home. I hope we'll enjoy many happy years together there." His voice was rich with emotion as he spoke.

"To Michelle, your new job and home." Peggy and Carson repeated the toast, lifting their glasses and touching Cale's.

Michelle was stunned into silence by his words. Cale loved her. He admitted it to her in front of his parents, so he must be serious. Wild joy rocketed through her with the realization she loved him back. Whatever it was she had felt for Rob was a pale candle compared to the fireworks of emotion she was experiencing at the moment. Cale tightened his fingers on hers, and she smiled brightly, her eyes misting with tears of happiness.

"To the man I love, our new home, and our future together," Michelle said breathlessly as she raised her glass and joined in the toast with her family.

## Chapter Eighteen

It was almost dusk when Michelle finished the chores. "Happy New Year," she called to the horses as she flicked off the light and latched the barn door. The first stars shone in the pale blue evening sky as the molten ball of the sun kissed the rolling hills to the west. Yellow light spilled from the kitchen windows across the yard. Peggy was putting together a light supper before they'd head into Doc and Mary's for the night's celebrations. Michelle did a little skip and dance, whirling around in the last slanted light of the sun. It was her first New Year's Eve with Cale, a thrill of excitement spiraled through her gut. What a difference a year could make.

She glanced across the coulee where the lights of her childhood home shone in the gathering darkness. It looked like every light in the house was on, she giggled, George would have a fit when he got the hydro bill. She shook her head, who knew what George and his blond bimbo were up to. *Be nice, Michelle.* She cautioned herself, it's the holidays, after all. Dismissing her annoying brother and his latest conquest from her thoughts she bounded up the steps and into the mud room. Shedding her barn clothes, she stepped into the warmth of the kitchen. Carson and Cale had commandeered the harvest table. Every inch was covered with drawings and blueprints, the two men had their heads close together discussing some obscure aspects of the plumbing and heating Michelle would rather not know about. Peggy looked up as she came and grinned at her over the men's heads.

Michelle washed her hands at the sink and turned to help Cale's mom put the last few sandwiches on the plate. Peggy ladled steaming tomato soup into the waiting bowls on the counter.

"C'mon, boys. Time to eat, clear that mess away," she ordered.

Michelle grinned when the men obediently folded and stacked the paperwork. Carson gathered it all up and placed it on the small desk by the phone.

"They're so well trained, Peggy. I'm impressed," Michelle joked.

"Start 'em young," the older woman replied failing to keep an amused smile from spreading across her face.

"Nothin' to do with training, I'll have you know. When there's food involved you don't have to ask this cowboy twice to clear the table." Carson winked at his wife.

Cale shook his head and smoothed out the rumpled tablecloth. Michelle brought the platter of sandwiches while Cale's parents carried the bowls of soup to the table. She reached for a soup spoon from the glass spooner sitting in its usual place in the middle of the table. A thrill of awareness shot through her when Cale's fingers brushed against hers as he snagged a utensil at the same time. Michelle blushed hotly at the knowing look that passed between his parents. She snatched her hand back and took a seat across from him. *Since when does picking up a spoon qualify as foreplay?* Fear reared its head for a moment, what if this didn't work out with Cale? Her chest tightened and it was hard to draw air into her lungs. Swallowing a mouthful of soup seemed to ease the physical discomfort, but the doubt just wouldn't go away. He's not Rob, he's not Rob, Michelle repeated the mantra to herself.

"Are you okay, dear?" Peggy placed a hand on her arm. "You look like you've just seen a ghost."

"No, no, I'm fine, really." Michelle smiled at the woman, but avoided Cale's concerned gaze. "Just excited about tonight, I think. It's been a long time since Mary invited this many people for New Year's Eve." She raised her head to find Cale regarding her with a puzzled and wary expression on his handsome face. Shaking her head and giving him a tiny smile, she applied herself to the food on her plate.

Supper dishes cleaned and put away, Michelle followed the Benjamins out to their truck. Cale held the door for her and climbed in behind her. After securing the seatbelt he laced his fingers with hers and squeezed.

"No money business back there, you two," Carson teased.

"Carson! They not children for heaven's sake," Peggy responded.

"It's okay, Dad. I'll keep the heavy breathing to a minimum. I wouldn't want to offend your sensibilities with my wild behaviour," Cale bantered back.

Michelle stared out the window to hide the tide of red she could feel creeping up her face. She hardly knew these people. They were going to think she was a sex maniac or something. Cale was making it sound like they went at it like rabbits, for heaven's sake.

"Smile, Chelly. It's just harmless teasing," Cale whispered. "Dad likes to give me a hard time, but he doesn't mean anything by it."

Peggy inserted a CD in the player and started singing along. Michelle joined in, glad of the diversion. Before she knew it, they were pulling up to Doc's. Cars and trucks filled the small lot in front of the clinic and spilled out onto the narrow street.

"My stars, Mary must have invited the whole town," Michelle exclaimed.

"Looks like," Peggy agreed.

Carson wedged the big Dodge crew cab into a parking space down the street and turned off the ignition. Michelle opened the door and jumped down, Cale close behind her. She threw her head back to gaze at the blanket of stars above. Cale's arms came around her and she leaned back against him, his breath warm as he kissed her ear.

"It's a beautiful night, isn't it," she said.

"Not as beautiful as the woman in my arms." He tightened his hold.

"C'mon, you two love birds. Quit canoodling in the middle of the street," Carson called.

Grinning, Michelle let Cale lead her up the steps and in the front door. There was a small vestibule which was overflowing with coats and boots. The holidays were the only time the front door was ever used. It meant Mary was going overboard and outdoing herself to throw a shindig to be remembered.

"Happy New Year!" Mary sailed across the living room, a headband with shiny stars and sparkly horns adorned with flashing lights on her grey curls. She hugged Michelle and then Cale.

"Peggy, it's been too long," she greeted Cale's mom. "How is Dolores? I haven't heard from her in a donkey's age. Carson, handsome as always, good to see you, boy" Without waiting for a response, she took Peggy's hand and towed her across the room to where Doc was holding court in his favorite chair.

Michelle grinned up at Cale and laughed out loud at the forlorn look on Carson's face. Mary in full hostess mode was a force to be reckoned with.

"Seems I've been deserted. Think I'll just go find me a drink." Carson ambled over to the bar set up in the kitchen.

"Do you want something?" Cale asked.

"Maybe some white wine, for a change."

"Be right back, don't go away." He winked and wended his way through the crowd toward the kitchen.

Michelle found a clear space and perched on the arm of the sofa. Her gaze roamed the roomful of guests, looked like just about everyone from town and the surrounding area was there. Mary's annual New Year's Eve party was legendary, although it appeared she had really out done herself this time. The house was so packed with people it was hard to move, someone had thrown open the front and back doors to get some fresh air into the overheated atmosphere. George's dark head caught her attention as the crowd parted for a moment. He had his arms securely around Stacey's shoulders and was smiling down at her. A couple of his old girlfriends were looking daggers at the pair of them. *This might prove to be a very interesting night.* Amy Sargent was known for her volatile temper and right now, if looks could kill, Stacey would be French fried. *Wonder how Georgie plans to handle that?*

"Here you go."

Cale's voice at her elbow startled her so much she almost slid off her perch. "Thanks. Oh, oh, looks like Amy is headed George's way. This should be interesting."

"What do you mean? Is she one of his old girlfriends?"

"Not so old. They were thick as thieves all last summer. He kinda just disappeared on her with no explanation." Michelle giggled at the trapped expression on her brother's face as he saw the woman bearing down on him. Mary, quick as always to head off any explosions that might mar her festivities, intercepted her just as she reached the couple. Taking her firmly in hand, Mary turned her toward a huddle of young people which included some single men. *Trust Mary to bail George out.*

"Mission accomplished, bomb defused," Cale remarked. "That woman does have a knack for arranging things."

"I don't think anyone has every outsmarted our Miss Mary. Doc says he never had a chance once she set her hat for him. Before he knew it he was squashed into a monkey suit and sweating it out at the front of the church waiting on her to come up the aisle," Michelle's voice was full of laughter.

"Happy New Year!" Rob stood in the doorway with Kayla beside him.

"Same to you, young fella." Doc made his way through the crowd to shake his hand. "Good to see you. You too, Kayla." He drew them into the room, steering them to the far side away from Michelle and Cale.

"Looks like Mary isn't the only one running interference tonight." Cale looked down at her thoughtfully.

"No need. I'm not gonna rip her hair out or anything. She's welcome to him, the rat bastard." Michelle stood up. "Did I tell you he wants her to get pregnant, like yesterday?" She plunged on when Cale shook his head. "She

254

showed up at the door a couple of days ago, looking for him. Like I'd let him in…Anyway, he wants kids right away and she wants to wait. We were just the opposite, I wanted a house full of babies and all he wanted was to run the roads chasing his rodeo dreams."

"What did you tell her?"

She snorted. "I told her to go drag him out of whatever bar he was in and set him down and work it out. Maybe he'll listen to her better'n he did to me."

"How come you never mentioned this before?"

"I forgot about it in the rush to get the house ready for your parents. It wasn't that important."

"You sure about that?"

"Yeah, of course." She rounded on him. "Why do you think I'm keeping secrets or something?" Anger coloured her words.

"I hope not, Chelly. I don't want to think that. Just seems odd you never thought to mention she dropped by."

"It just slipped my mind. I didn't think it was that important. Can we just drop it for now?"

"Sure. I'm gonna go get another beer, do you want anything?"

Michelle set her empty wine glass on the mantle and shook her head. The last thing she needed was to get all muzzy headed and stupid in front of his parents. Her gaze followed the tall form as Cale made his way through the crowd, stopping to talk with clients along the way.

Peggy appeared at Michelle's elbow. "It's so nice to see Mary and Luke again. I haven't seen them in ages. Mom keeps us updated on what's going on, but it's not the same as a visit."

"I'm glad you're having a good time." Michelle smiled at the older woman.

"It's good to see Cale so happy. He's always been so intense and focussed on his career, it nice to see him relax a bit. You're good for him, I hope you'll be joining our family officially soon," Peggy said.

"Thanks, he makes me happy, too. I don't know about anything official, though. We haven't even talked about anything like that."

"They say action speaks louder than words, dear. I'd say he's pretty committed to your relationship."

"What about Stacey? Was he ever serious with her?" She hated herself for asking, but curiosity got the better of her.

"Stacey chased after him for a while, but he never gave her a second look that way. They were good friends and that's all it ever was. Besides, it looks like she's set her sights on your brother. Are you okay with that?" Peggy tilted her head toward the couple by the kitchen door.

"So long as he keeps her claws out of Cale, I'm fine with it. I warned her to be careful about George, he's the love 'em and leave 'em type."

"Well, I'm hoping there'll be something shiny on your finger before too long. It's time my son settled down and gave me some grandbabies." Peggy stood up with a smile and went to join her husband.

Michelle got up as well. Suddenly restless, she slipped through the crowd and out onto the back porch off the kitchen. The cold air nipped her nose, though it was a welcome relief from the close atmosphere inside. Stars winked brightly in the sable velvet sky. She took a deep breath and released it in a cloud of white frost. *Is Cale thinking of asking me to marry him? Do I want him to? Damn, I'm scared. I like him way too much already, what'll I do if he decides to dump me?*

"Penny for your thoughts." Rob blocked the light from the kitchen door. He stepped out onto the porch and closed the door behind him before coming to stand beside her.

"Where's Kayla?"

He waved vaguely toward the house. "In there somewhere, talkin' to Mom. Forget her, it's you I want to talk to."

Michelle took a step back and studied his face. "You're pissed, Rob. Go back in the house and find your wife." When he didn't move, she started to push past him, stopping abruptly when he grabbed her arm.

"Let me go, Rob." Her voice was dangerously quiet.

"I'm sorry, Chelly. I made a mistake. I love you. I know you love me, too. You always have, ever since we were kids." The words were slurred and he swayed on his feet, his eyes slightly unfocussed.

"Let me go, Rob. You're drunker than a skunk. You married Kayla, remember? I'm going back in the house now, you should find Kayla and go home to sleep it off." His grip loosened for a second and Michelle tried to pull free. Rob cursed and yanked her against him. Rough whiskers scraped her cheek as he kissed her possessively. Michelle shoved at his shoulders, but then was forced to hang on to him as the idiot staggered and almost fell. His hands gripped her face, holding her lips to his. His tongue probed her taut mouth seeking entrance.

"C'mon, Chelly. You know you want me. This used to turn you on, remember?" He twisted his hand in her hair to hold her head steady and grabbed her other hand and pressed it against his erection. "See how much I want you, darlin'? Kayla doesn't have to know…one more time for old time's sake…you know you want it…"

"What the hell…" Cale stood in the doorway, his face a thundercloud as he met her startled gaze. His eyes swept over her, from her kiss swollen lips to her hand on Rob's bulging jeans. "Let me know when you're finished, it's almost midnight." He turned on his heel and stomped away before Michelle could utter a word.

"Let me go!" She ground her teeth and wrenched her hand away from his grip. When Rob was drunk he didn't have the sense of a gopher in the middle of the road. He shoved his mouth down on hers again and palmed her breast.

"God damn it, Rob. Leave off!" Michelle dug her fingers into his wrist to loosen the grip on her hair and brought her knee up hard between his spread legs. He dropped to the floor boards with a curse, clutching his groin. Michelle stepped over him and opened the kitchen door. She paused on the threshold to look back. "Don't you ever touch me again. Do you hear me?" Without waiting for a response she stormed into the house.

Cries of Happy New Year rang in her ears. A glance at the clock showed the two hands upright on the twelve. *Great, just great. Where is Cale?* She ventured into the living room where Mary was at the piano leading the singing of Auld Lang Syne. Doc caught Michelle up in huge hug and planted a kiss on her forehead.

"You smell like cigarette smoke and booze, what have you been up to?" Doc held her at arm's length and studied her face.

"Fending off Rob, the jack ass. Kayla needs to get that idiot home before he does more damage."

"What did he do? Do I need to kick his ass?" Doc glanced around the room.

"He decided he needed a little bit of what he threw away. He's drunker than a skunk and started pawing me, Cale came out and saw us. Heaven only knows what he thought was going on and he didn't wait around to find out." Her breath caught in her throat as tears threatened. "I left Rob rolling around on the floor of the porch. It's gonna hurt to ride for a while." An evil grin crossed her face.

"Michelle, what happened?" Peggy stood at her elbow. "Cale come through here like the devil was at his heels. Said he was going back to the ranch."

"We came together, how's he getting home?" Michelle looked about wildly, trying to find his dark head above the crowd.

"George lent him his truck. Said something about understanding how a man needed to get away from you at times. Cale grabbed the keys and left without saying good bye. What the hell happened?"

"Rob happened." Michelle sighed. "He decided it was time for a reunion and wouldn't take no for an answer until I practically gelded him. Cale walked in on it and didn't wait around for an explanation. I need to find him."

"Kayla, darlin'. You been lookin' fer me?" Rob reeled into the room, bouncing off the door frame. "Wanna go get ridden hard and put away wet? Shake theme pretty boobies for me…"

The sudden silence in the room was deafening. Kayla stalked across to her husband and stopped in front of him. The sharp crack of her hand on his face halted his tirade. "Don't you ever speak to me like that again, do you hear me?" she hissed. "Do you think I don't know you were out there hitting on your ex?"

As amusing as it was to see Rob getting his comeuppance, Michelle turned to Doc. "Can I borrow your truck? I need to talk to Cale, it can't wait."

"Sure Chelly." He dug in his pocket and pressed the keys into her hand. "Make sure you say goodbye to Mary, though or she'll have my head."

"Thanks, Doc." She kissed him on the cheek. "I'll make it right with Cale, Peggy. I promise." She slipped through the crowd to Mary's side. Giving her a hug, she whispered in her ear. "I'm gonna go find Cale and straighten this out. Damn Rob, the idiot should never touch a drop."

"You go, girl. Don't let that boy get away. He's the real deal."

"I know, Mary. I know."

She ran lightly down the back steps and jumped in Doc's old truck. Tapping her fingers impatiently on the steering wheel she waited for the glow plug to go out. Finally, it winked out and she slid the truck into gear. Damn Rob to hell and back. What was wrong with the man? You'd think he'd learn by now he couldn't have his cake and eat it, too. The back end of the truck slewed sideways as she turned onto the main road. Sweat gathered on her brow, curling her hair into tendrils. Michelle rolled the window down, faint sounds of revelry sounded in the night. How far ahead of her was he? Pressing harder on the accelerator, she sent the vehicle down the deserted stretch of highway.

Frost glimmered on the pavement and the stars shone overhead. It was a beautiful night, how did things go so wrong? Damn Rob, damn his ass all the way to hell.

Michelle gulped in deep breaths of the frigid air blowing in the window. It did nothing to calm her rising panic. *What if he doesn't believe me? What if he thinks I wanted that ass wipe to kiss me?* For once, she was too angry to cry. Rob was not going to ruin the best thing that ever happened to her, just because he couldn't keep his dick in his pants once he had a few drinks in him. The turn for the ranch road flashed by, cursing she jammed on the brakes and reversed down the highway. Punching the throttle, she raised rooster tails of snow as the truck careened down the dirt road. Red tail lights glimmered ahead of her, she was almost on the vehicle before she realized it was pulled over to the shoulder. Yanking the wheel, she skidded by.

Damn, that's Cale's truck! Michelle stomped on the brake sending the truck into a three-sixty skid. Grimly, she wrestled the wheel, fighting for control. Doc would kill her dead if she hurt his old truck. Finally it lurched to a stop skewed sideways on the road. Michelle dropped her head against her hands still clutching the wheel. Her breathing hadn't steadied before the cab door was wrenched open.

"What the hell are you trying to do, kill yourself?" Cale glared at her, his breathing as ragged as her own. "Michelle? What are you doing here?" His expression became wary as he realized who it was.

"Looking for you. What are you doing parked in the middle of the road, for heaven's sake?"

"It's not the middle of the road, you were going way too fast. I'm way off on the shoulder. Whose truck did you steal?"

"Doc lent it to me so I could find you and explain." She stopped talking as a closed shuttered look froze his features.

"Nothing to explain. It was pretty obvious what was going on. If you aren't hurt, I'll just head back to the house." He turned and walked back toward his truck.

"Cale, it isn't like that," she called after him. When he didn't stop, she jumped out of the cab and ran after him. Catching up with him, she grabbed his arm and spun him toward her. "Listen to me, won't you. I wasn't kissing him—"

"And your hand wasn't down his pants? Give me a break, Michelle." He pulled free and got into the truck, slamming the door in her face.

"Cale..." she paused at the thunderous look on his face.

"Move Doc's truck so I can get by, or so help me I'll ram it," he ordered.

"Cale, please —" she began again.

"Now! Move it!" He put his vehicle in gear and left her standing in the gravel.

"Ass wipe," she muttered. Stomping back to Doc's truck, she passed Cale's window without glancing his way. She got in the pickup and maneuvered it in the loose gravel until it was pointed in the right direction again. Cale flashed by her, rocks and stones pinging off her fenders as he did. Jamming the truck into gear, she followed him back to the house. He was going to listen to her if she had to hogtie him. With any luck, his parents wouldn't come home before they had hashed this nonsense out. *Damn Rob, egotistical ass wipe. What did I ever see in him?*

# Chapter Nineteen

Michelle pulled up and parked beside Cale. He slammed his door and stalked toward the house without looking at her. She hurried after him, catching up with him by the back door. He glared at her over his shoulder.

"Go away, Michelle. I don't want you here."

"Where am I supposed to go?"

"Go stay at Rob's, eat crow and beg George to take you in. I don't care."

"I'm not going anywhere until you listen to me." She pushed her way into the house behind him.

"Honestly Michelle, I've had enough. I'm too tired to talk about this right now. I'm tired of wondering if you really want a life with me or you're just rebounding from Rob. If he crooked his finger would you go running back to him...I guess I got my answer tonight. Didn't I?" His voice was bitter and defeated. "Just go away." He moved across the dark kitchen without turning on a light and disappeared down the hall.

"Cale, why won't you listen to me? I need to explain what happened. It's not what you think..." Her voice failed her at the sight of him storming back down the hall toward her, barely suppressed anger in every line of his body.

"It wasn't you with his tongue down your throat, it wasn't you with your hand down his pants, it wasn't his hand pawing at you? What wasn't it, Michelle. Go on, tell me." Cale challenged her.

Michelle gulped and wet her lips. "I went outside to get some air. Rob came out and he was pissed to the gills. I told him to screw off and tried to back in the house and look for you. He grabbed me and started kissing me. I didn't kiss him back, I didn't..." She paused at the unyielding expression on his face. "I didn't, he had me by the hair and grabbed my hand, he forced me to touch him. Right after you left, I kneed him in the balls and left him rolling on the porch. Ask Doc. I ran in the house looking for you, Doc said you left in hurry, borrowed George's truck. I came after you...I love you, Cale. Not Rob. I don't know what I ever saw in that ass wipe. You've got to believe me..."

"Why should I believe you? Ever since I've known you, you've been mooning after that bastard. Even though he's married now you can't keep your hands off him. What kind of person are you?" Disgust laced his tones.

"I'm so done with him. You have to see that. He was drunk, when he's liquored up he thinks anything female will lie down and spread her legs for him. It's you I want, Cale. Now and forever..."

Annoyance flared across his face at the buzz of his cell phone. He dug in the pocket of his shirt and answered it, his gaze never leaving her.

"Dr. Benjamin." His brows drew together as he listened to the caller in silence. "Fine, Dad. See you in the morning." He ended the call. "Mom and Dad are staying in town for the night. Mom thinks Dad's had too much to drink and she doesn't like to drive in the dark." He turned back to the hall. "You should go," he said over his shoulder.

Michelle sank down on a chair at the table. "Why won't you believe me? You said you loved me, but you obviously don't trust me. Love is nothing without trust, I know that now."

Cale stood stock still in the hallway, his back still turned to her. When he didn't speak or move, she got to her feet. "Okay, I'm leaving. If you can't trust me, you can't really love me. I'm glad I found out now before I got in any deeper. Good bye, Cale. I'll come and get the horses and chickens once I figure out where I'm staying. I'll get Storm and the puppies into the truck."

Defeated, she got to her feet and bent to collect the sleeping puppies. Storm whined deep in her throat, her body trembling. Michelle dropped to her knees and hugged her. "It's okay, dog. We'll be fine, you'll see." Placing the last puppy in the kennel she closed the door and straightened up.

Cale still stood in the hallway with his back to her. Michelle gave him one last look and picked up the kennel. Storm hopped along at her side as she left the kitchen. Tears blurred her vision and it was a chore to get the heavy kennel into the truck. A final heave set it in place. She closed the door and opened the passenger door for Storm. Michelle put a hand under her bum to assist her into the cab. She stumbled around the front of the truck and got in the driver side. She shoved the key in the ignition but didn't turn it. Laying her head down on the steering wheel she let the tears come as they would.

Her head came up with a jerk at a tap on the window. Wiping her eyes, she rolled the window down. "What do you want?"

"You forgot the puppy food." Cale handed her a bag but seemed reluctant to leave.

"Thanks," she mumbled taking the bag of food. She set it on the seat and turned the key in the ignition.

"Michelle, wait..." He reached into the truck and touched her cheek.

She twisted away and refused to look at him. Her hand twitched on the gear shift but somehow she couldn't bring herself to slide it into reverse.

"Don't go. Come back in the house..."

"And do what, Cale? You don't trust me, no matter how often you say you love me, you don't trust me. There's nothing else to say." Her voice came out thin and strangled. She swallowed past the huge lump in her throat.

The pickup door flew open and he hauled her bodily out of the seat. His grip was strong on her shoulders and if she was honest with herself, she didn't really want to break free.

"Look at me, Chelly," he commanded gently.

Unwillingly, she raised her eyes from their contemplation of his shirt buttons. Starlight gleamed on his seal black hair and reflected bright pin points in his dark eyes. Michelle blinked and looked closer at his face, his cheeks were shiny with tear tracks.

"Hell, Michelle. I don't know what to think. Can you blame me for jumping to conclusions? Just about everyone in town has warned me about your obsession with Rob, warned me not to get too close. And then I walk out the door and find you in his arms..."

"It wasn't like that," she defended herself. "I was trying to get away, but he was so drunk if I hadn't held him up we'd both have ended up in Mary's rose bushes. I don't love him anymore. I'm not sure what we had was ever love in the first place. I didn't ask him to follow me out onto the porch for God's sake."

Cale pulled her roughly against him, his shoulders shook and tremors ran through his chest under her fingers. "It's not that I don't trust you, I guess maybe I don't think I can be the man you want. I'm not wild and carefree like Rob, I've got a demanding job and sometimes it seems like it comes before anything else. I thought you were bored with me already and went looking for some excitement. I'm sorry, Michelle. I should have listened to your explanation." His voice was muffled in her hair.

Her chest hurt so bad she wondered if she was having a heart attack. Of their own accord, her arms came up around his waist. "If it was Rob or anyone else I was after why would I high tail it after you? I love you, but sometimes love isn't enough. If you don't trust me…"

Cale stopped her words by covering her mouth with his. With a shuddering sigh of surrender, Michelle leaned into his embrace.

"Will you come back in the house now? I'm freezing to death out here." He lifted his head and a tiny smile tugged at the corner of his mouth.

Dropping her head against his chest, Michelle wrestled with her pride. She hated he had jumped to conclusions about Rob, but was it a deal breaker? Was she willing to live her life without him in it? Gramma's advice rang in her ears: *Ain't nothing that can't be fixed if you love each other enough.* Like magic, all the pieces fell into place. What she felt for Cale deserved a chance to grow. "You get the puppy crate and I'll get Storm."

Cale hugged her so tight she squeaked a bit. He released her and went to fetch the crate from the back seat of the crew cab. Michelle lifted Storm down and followed him into the house. She stood awkwardly in the doorway as the black dog brushed past her and flopped down on her bed by the stove. Cale set the crate down and opened the door for the babies, they slept on in a bundle of black fur, oblivious to the drama playing out over their heads.

He crossed the floor and took her hands, drawing Michelle into the room. "I don't know what to say. How do we go forward from here?" She searched his face.

Cale surprised her by letting go of her hand and digging in the pocket of his jeans. "How's this?" He held out a small red organza pouch. When Michelle didn't respond, he turned her hand over and dropped it in her palm. She fumbled with the satin ribbons holding it closed. A diamond ring fell into her hand. "Will you marry me, Michelle? Maybe I should have asked Doc's permission seeing as your dad is gone, but it's kinda like closing the barn door after the horse is free…" His voice trailed off. "Michelle?"

She raised her gaze to meet his. "Is that like saying 'Why buy the cow when you can get the milk for free'?"

"I didn't mean it like that, for God's sake woman." He raked a hand through his hair. "I only meant…well…we've already slept together and this isn't 1963…"

"I know, sweetie. I was only teasing you. Yes, I will marry you on one condition."

"What?" His tone was wary.

"You never run out on me again and you promise to always listen to my side of things before you go off have cocked."

A brilliant smile lit his features. "Deal!" Cale pulled her into his arms and kissed her soundly. "Here, let me put that on for you. Does it fit?" He slid the gold band onto her finger, the three diamonds winking in the light.

"It's like it was made for me? How did you know what size?" Michelle twisted the ring on her finger.

"I didn't. It was my great grandmother's. I asked Dad to bring it with him. I had it in my hand when I went looking for you and found you with Rob. I'm sorry I overreacted, Michelle." He ran a hand over his face. "It was like my worst nightmare coming true and I felt like an idiot standing there with an engagement ring in my hand and you had your hand...well you know…"

"Oh, Cale. I'm sorry, too. But, you should have stuck around a few minutes longer. I nailed the idiot in the nuts with my knee and then Kayla went up one side of him and down the other when he staggered back into the living room."

"I don't want to talk about them anymore tonight. Just us. Do you want a long engagement or do you want to get married soon?"

She tilted her head to the side and grinned up at him. "How about in the spring? Maybe May, when the prairie crocus are in bloom?"

"I think I can wait that long." A slow smile spread across his face.

"Well, seeing as the horse is already out of the barn as you so eloquently put it, there's no reason why we can't go ahead and anticipate the wedding, as Grandpa would say."

Cale kissed the top of her head, took her hand and flicked the light out as they left the kitchen. "Happy New Year, Michelle."

"Happy New Year, Cale," she echoed as she followed him down the dark hall to his bed.

Storm heaved a huge sigh and rested her head on her paws. All was right with the world.

## The End

Nancy Bell books published by
Books We Love Ltd.

### Young Adult Fantasy

**Laurel's Quest – The Cornwall Adventures Book 1**

**A Step Beyond - The Cornwall Adventures Book**

**Go Gently - The Cornwall Adventures Book 3**

## About the Author

Nancy Marie Bell is a proud Albertan and lives near Balzac, Alberta with her husband and various critters. She is a member of The Writers Union of Canada and the Writers Guild of Alberta. Nancy has numerous writing credits to her name, having three novels published and her work has been published in various magazines. She has also had her work recognized and honoured with various awards, and most recently, a silver medal in the Creative Writing category of the Alberta 55 Plus Summer Games in 2013. Nancy has presented at the Surrey International Writers Conference in 2012 and 2013, and at the Writers Guild of Alberta Conference in 2014. She has publishing credits in poetry, fiction and non-fiction.